SARAH'

TARYN'S CAMERA BOOK 9

REBECCA PATRICK-HOWARD

WANT MORE?

Want access to FREE books (audio, print, and digital), prizes, and new releases before anyone else? Then sign up for Rebecca's VIP mailing list. She promises she won't spam you!

Click here to sign up! http://eepurl.com/Srwkn

For Sara
and her house

ONE

Sara's House, RPH (Cooper House, Lexington, Kentucky)

*T*he house behind her was alive.

From where she sat on the broken front porch of the rambling farm house, she could hear the sounds of the past behind her.

1

Rather than feeling afraid, however, Taryn Magill was comforted.

Over the course of the past few years she'd grown if not accustomed to, then at least familiar with, the ghosts that haunted her life and followed her from job to job. An artist, she'd spent her adult life creating renderings of old, decrepit buildings that were on the verge of falling down or being bulldozed. With her paints and brushes, she brought them back to life for her clients, creating realistic depictions of the poor old souls in their glory days.

Her beloved camera, Miss Dixie, had stuck with her through every project, helping her capture the details of the buildings–details she'd later use in the paintings themselves. Although her jobs had taken her all over the country, it had been a quiet, even peaceful existence, for the most part. That is, until Miss Dixie started picking up on scenes from the past.

Suddenly, where her eyes had showed her a vacant room with dusty floors and stringy cobwebs, Miss Dixie revealed a stunning parlor, complete with grand piano and sparkling crystal chandelier. The past had not remained static in those images, either. Eventually, those who had gone before her had reemerged as well, seeking answers and closure to their passing. She'd helped where she could, although not every story had seen a happy ending.

But what she heard behind her now was *not* restless spirits roaming around her aunt's foyer and living room. Rather, she was hearing the reassuring sounds of a house she'd known all her life–the settling of the creaky foundation, the wind rattling the old storm windows, the tree branches softly scraping against the bricks, and the muted country music drifting from the old record player to find her relaxing on the cool, autumn night.

Taryn had learned many things over the past few years, but the biggest and most important was that the past never truly died. While you couldn't necessarily go back and relive it, you *could* find yourself caught up in its essence if you let yourself. These days, Taryn found herself wanting to return more and more.

Now, if she closed her eyes, she could almost hear her aunt clanging around in the kitchen, could practically smell the spicy cinnamon rolls wafting past the foyer. With her eyes closed, she could see herself as a young girl again, her hair hanging in tangled red braids, her knees scuffed and bruised from climbing a tree.

Oh, Taryn thought, *to be young again.*

Most of the time she wanted to return to a distant past, to see turn-of-the-century New York City or to witness an ostentatious southern ball on a humid summer night. Tonight, however, she would have been happy just returning to a time when she was a little girl, waiting for her aunt to join her on the porch, knowing that she was in a safe place where she was loved and wanted.

Considering all that had happened over the past few months, for a few moments Taryn allowed herself to wallow in a bout of self-pity. Then the oven timer went off, its shrill alarm slicing through the New England breeze, announcing the readiness of her frozen pizza. Groaning, she stood and dusted off the seat of her pants. The porch was sloping to one side–one more thing she needed to fix.

"Add it to the list," Taryn muttered as she turned and started back inside the house.

The door had slammed shut behind her and she was halfway to the kitchen before the blackness filled the space she'd left behind. From a distance, it might have been a shadow–the result of a dark cloud passing over the moon. Up close, however, it was solid and greasy and not truly black at all–blues, greens, and yellows swirled together in an oily residue. Up close, the scent was putrid–rotten and spoiled meat. The smell not just of death, but of decay and hate.

*　　　*　　　*

TARYN'S CLOSET MADE HER SAD. On one side hung an eclectic mix of her aunt's pastel business suits and gardening clothes–a sad reminder that she was no longer there to wear either of them. On the other side was a haphazard collection of her own once impressive, but now shrunken, wardrobe–a sad reminder of what she'd lost in the tornado.

Taryn took a moment to mourn the loss of her once-grand collection of vintage dresses, cowboy boots, and Betsey Johnson purses. She hadn't spent a ton of money on her clothes, but she'd collected them from all over the country and had spent years lovingly growing her collection piece by piece. She didn't have children or pets–she'd had cardigans and shoes.

"You're lucky," she chastised herself now, mimicking the neighbor from across the hall who had stood with her in the parking lot, watching Taryn's building go up in flames.

And, to a point, Taryn *was* lucky. After all, she'd been at the cinema when the tornado had hit, not at home. She hadn't been inside when the winds had blown off the roof like it was nothing but aluminum foil or when something had sparked an electrical fire, creating a blazing inferno in what had once been her living room.

She'd been lucky that, since the building's washer and dryer were broken at the time, she'd taken a handful of her favorite things to the dry cleaners and because she'd just returned from a project and hadn't yet unpacked her car, she'd had a trunk full of suitcases.

Yay for being lazy, Taryn thought wryly to herself now.

She knew that there were those who were much worse off than her but it didn't mean that she couldn't be bitter once in awhile. Matt had taught her how to back up her digital files, thank goodness, so she still had access to all her photos and music on the Cloud. And then there was the storage unit across town that still housed Andrew's things.

Of course, she hadn't opened *that* in many years and none of it felt like hers anymore.

Taryn had basically lost nearly everything she owned.

She'd spent two weeks at a local hotel, fighting with the insurance company and attempting to pick up the pieces to her life.

And then her transmission had gone out. Naturally, it had gone out while she was driving down Broadway on a Friday night, thus backing up downtown Nashville traffic for three blocks. Luckily, some of the inebriated partiers filing out of Tootsie's in between sets had taken pity on her plight and had happily helped her move her poor little car to the side of the road until the tow truck arrived.

Then, of course, there was the reason she'd been at the cinema the day of the tornado instead of at her apartment to begin with: Taryn had been breaking up with her boyfriend, Matt.

Okay, so "breaking up" might have been too strong a phrase, especially considering that they'd never officially agreed that they were dating in the first place. Still, for the past few years neither had dated anyone else, they spent all their free time with each other (despite the entire state of Georgia literally dividing them), and they'd occasionally talked of a more permanent future with one another. Moreover, they'd been friends for more than twenty years. He was her *best* friend and what sometimes felt like her only one.

Telling him that they both needed to move on had been the hardest thing she'd ever done—and she'd buried who she still considered to be the love of her life. And now, as she sifted through her meager closet to find a bathrobe of some sort in her Aunt Sarah's belongings, she was deathly afraid that the decision had been a terribly bad one—one she'd almost certainly regret for the rest of her life.

However short that may be.

TWO

Sara's House, RPH (Cooper House, Lexington, Kentucky)

At *one time the farm house had boasted* a whole other section. There had been three additional bedrooms, a small balcony on the second floor, and a pantry. A fire had taken care of those things long before Taryn, or her family, had come to the house.

8

Still, even without those things the house was large; it was much more house than Taryn was used to. But although she rambled around inside, basically a ghost herself as she slipped through the noiseless rooms, she didn't mind the size. Taryn loved old houses–the bigger, the better. She'd never met an old house she didn't like. Abandoned, neglected, fallen in, missing a wing, crumbling wallpaper, crumbling foundation–she loved them all. Her grandmother had lived in an old farm house outside of Nashville and Taryn had spent a lot of her time there growing up. That might have been where she'd learned to love the past. There were few things Taryn had loved more than waking up each morning and hearing her nana in the kitchen, the hard wood floor cool under her bare feet as she raced down the stairs to meet the new day. Taryn had grown up in a regular looking house in a regular looking subdivision that looked like every other development around town. It had been very uninspiring to a young girl with such a vivid imagination.

Now, she had an old house of her own.

"This old place has a personality," Sarah had often told Taryn as she'd followed her aunt around, helping her weed her garden or dust off seats of old, wooden furniture inside. "All buildings do, once they reach a certain age. It's as though they grow a soul watching the years roll by."

As a child, she'd spent quite a bit of time at her aunt's New Hampshire home. She'd loved those times with her, had wished for them to come more quickly. And, for a time, she'd been a regular visitor there. But then something had changed, and she'd stopped returning. Her parents, never ones to spend much time talking to her and now deceased so they were unable, hadn't told her why. Her grandmother had been darkly quiet about the matter.

As an adult, Taryn had tried to keep in touch with Sarah. They'd exchanged Christmas cards and the occasional phone call but although Taryn had the best of intentions she'd never made it back to New England to visit her again.

And then she'd died.

Taryn was shocked to the core to find that Sarah'd left her house, her pride and joy, to her. It made sense, she supposed, since she was Sarah's only living relative. Still...it was almost as unexpected as her death.

"You need to sell it, cut your losses," everyone had insisted.

"That house needs far too much work."

"It's out in the middle of nowhere; there's nothing to *do* up there!"

"You don't know anything about restoring an old house!"

"It's a money pit!"

Those things were probably true. It *did* need a lot of work. She didn't know anything about restoring old houses. It was out in the middle of nowhere.

Still...

Taryn sighed and buttoned up her flannel coat all the way to her chin. The wool cap holding down her red hair was warm and snug against her head. It was meant to have been a warm day, but until the sun came out and pushed its way through the trees that encircled the property like a fortress, the air felt like winter.

Taryn's doctor down in Portsmouth had encouraged her to get as much exercise as she could stand every day. It wouldn't cure her, but it would help strengthen her muscles, which would help her joints, and stretching was good for pain relief.

Taryn had taken to going for walks down the hillside to the lake every day. It was fifteen minutes there and fifteen minutes back, and the return journey was all uphill. She didn't know how long she'd be able to do it; going up was becoming a problem and more and more she was finding herself feeling faint and nauseated, but she'd keep it up for as long as she could.

The leaves crunched under her heavy boots. She'd been shopping over in Conway at the outlet stores. A girl had to restock her closet, after all, and the trips into town were

11

fun. Sometimes she'd take in a movie while she was there or duck into one of the restaurants for dinner. Sarah's kitchen was the first thing she'd restored but she still wasn't using it as much as she should.

Matt had mostly done the cooking when they were together. He was a good cook and most women would've felt lucky to have someone like that in the kitchen. It had made Taryn lazy, though. She was just starting to get back in the habit again.

When she reached the bottom, the slate-gray lake unrolled before her, peaceful and still. The water barely seemed to move. There was a summer camp on the other side and back in July the valley had resonated with the sounds of children.

She'd enjoyed sitting on the bench she'd had brought in for herself and listening to the cries and shouts of laughter while she'd written in her journal or read. Now that school was back in session, it was impossibly quiet and downright lonely at times. Taryn was miles from the closest town; her small township had no stores to speak of and only a small gas station. Her father had referred to Sarah's house as living in the "New Hampshire wilderness" and he wasn't far off. She had to drive to neighboring Lewisboro for supplies. The only people that ever visited her was the housekeeper she'd hired, the palliative care worker that came once a week, and the mail man.

On *really* exciting days, they all came at the same time.

There was a big splash in the middle of the lake and it startled Taryn. She leaned forward and watched as the ripples moved outwards one by one, slowly traveling towards her. She had a sudden image of someone hiding underwater and steadily making their way to where she was sitting, ready to pop up and frighten her at the last second.

"I am losing my damn mind," Taryn laughed shakily. She stood and shook her head. "It's Sarah's fault."

Indeed, her aunt had often told her the story about the underground caves in the lake, about the treasures that were meant to be submerged under water. About the lake monster that was meant to reside there.

Taryn knew they were only stories, local legends, but for some reason she was feeling shaky that afternoon. She'd heard a mouse in the dining room when she'd first come down the back stairs that morning and she'd jumped a mile, nearly losing her balance and landing on her bottom. She should be stronger, she knew that; she'd certainly seen and heard enough over the past few years to strengthen her resolve.

Still, she was human–and a woman living in the mountains, in the *forest*, alone.

"I am a horror movie waiting to happen," Taryn sighed.

And, with that, she turned and began the slow ascent up the hillside. As she walked, she tried to ignore the feeling of penetrating eyes boring into her back, measuring her every step.

*　　*　　*

"I WAS AFRAID YOU'D KICKED THE BUCKET ON ME."

Taryn peered up from her pillow and grinned at the woman standing in front of her. Charaty was tall and almost dangerously thin, but the woman was as strong as an ox and didn't take any bullshit. Taryn had no idea how old she was. She could have been twenty-five or sixty. The woman was timeless. She thought she might be of Russian descent and she took her housework so seriously that she ran the job like the military. Taryn was almost certain that Charaty had been, if not a dictator, then at least a high-ranking general in a former life.

To be honest, she was a little afraid of her. Charaty came three times a week to clean and organize and Taryn found herself stressing before each scheduled visit, hoping she hadn't messed her work up from the last time *too* badly.

"I was just taking a little nap," Taryn apologized. "I was out walking around earlier and got tired."

"People die while they nap," Charaty sniffed loudly and regarded Taryn with little sympathy.

"Then at least I'll go doing something I love," Taryn chirped.

She thought the other woman might have cracked the slightest of a smile.

"They say how long you have?"

Charaty was blunt, but Taryn appreciated that about her. No beating around the bush. She'd been highly recommended around the township and although she occasionally made the hairs on the back of Taryn's neck stand at attention, she wasn't sorry she'd hired her.

"They don't know," Taryn replied. "Whenever this aneurysm decides to burst. We're trying to manage the pain to keep my blood pressure down. That's all we can do right now."

"And no surgery to fix it?" Charaty's voice softened for just an instant and Taryn saw sympathy in her eyes.

Taryn shook her head. "With my connective tissue disorder, the surgery would probably kill me straightaway. The tissue won't clamp anymore; it just disintegrates when they try to move it around. We discovered that when they had to remove half of my intestines earlier in the summer."

Taryn looked down and ruefully studied the colostomy bag attached to her jeans.

Sexy as hell, she thought to herself.

Charaty straightened and brushed an invisible strand of hair back from her face. "My cousin had an aneurysm. Overdid it out in the garden one day and just fell over dead."

"Oh." Taryn wasn't sure how she was meant to respond to that.

Charaty nodded. "Was three days before anyone found her. Good thing they had a cold front come through at the time or else the buzzards would've been there first."

With that, she turned and marched off through the house. Within minutes, Taryn could hear the roar of the vacuum cleaner on the Oriental rug in the parlor.

Ehlers-Danlos Syndrome. Five years ago, Taryn had not even heard of the connective tissue disorder that was now dominating her life. It was congenital, so she'd had it since birth, but she'd been in her early thirties before she'd started feeling its effects.

At first, it had been the severe headaches, the dizziness, and the occasional bouts of pain in her legs. Then had come the regular dislocations and subluxations of her joints. She'd roll over too hard in her sleep and dislocate a hip, cough too hard and pop out a rib.

The chronic pain had become progressively worse; there were days when she was unable to walk or stand for long periods of time. It became difficult to eat–she either threw up everything that went down or was hit by labor-like pains that took away any joy she once received from the food she consumed. In the past year she'd lost her gallbladder, left kidney, and a few feet of intestines simply because they'd ruptured and had to be removed. The EDS had given her cranio-cervio instability, meaning that her neck was no longer properly supporting her head. The neurological issues meant that it was difficult for her to remember certain things, to hold a paint brush steady anymore, or to feel hot and cold the way normal people did.

The real problem, however, was the aneurysm. For a while they'd simply watched it and waited, hoping it wouldn't grow. After all, people could have them for years and never know they were there. They didn't *have* to be a ticking time bomb. Hers was, of course. It had doubled in size in just under a year.

The rumble of Charaty's vacuum cleaner made it difficult for Taryn to concentrate on her nap.

"Who cares?" she asked the empty room. "It's not like I'll sleep tonight anyway."

17

For the past week she'd been up and down at all hours of the night, unable to sleep for more than an hour straight at any given time. She'd read just about every book in Sarah's house and watched all the old VHS tapes laying around. (Mostly "Murder, She Wrote" episodes and Bette Davis films.) She was going to have to find more to do. She was at a standstill with the house. All the major things had been done. And since her illness had made working impossible, she was feeling a little disjointed. Taryn had been working nonstop since high school; it felt odd to just give it all up. Her job really *was* her life.

Taryn was halfway out the door when Charaty called out to her. "The roof is looking fine!"

Taryn paused and turned. "Yeah, looks good, doesn't it? They finished after you left the other day."

The main thing was that the gaping hole over the screened-in back porch was gone and her bedroom no longer leaked buckets.

"You get ripped off?" Charaty demanded.

"I don't think so," Taryn laughed.

"Good," Charaty shouted. "You think you are, then you give me a call. I'll straighten it out for you."

Taryn laughed as the vacuum started up again behind her. Yep, she bet Charaty would "straighten it out" for her.

Too bad she didn't have someone like her to run her personal life, too.

*   *   *

OUTSIDE, THE WIND HOWLED AND SHRIEKED as it whipped around the corners of the house, chasing an invisible intruder like a devoted hound dog.

Taryn snuggled down under her comforter and turned the television's volume up. Sarah's house didn't get cable but she'd uncovered a DVD player that afternoon and now she had considerably more choices. She was currently binge-watching "Twin Peaks" and snacking on chocolate chip covered popcorn she'd made in her new kitchen. She thought Sarah would probably approve.

The house rattled around her. "It looks like it's gonna fall over but the foundation's still remarkably solid," the contractor had assured her on his first visit. It had needed work, of course, but the house had not been a lost cause.

Taryn reminded herself of this fact as she listened to it take a beating, listened as the house fought back. Perched atop a small rise in a field below the biggest mountain in the county, the house was surrounded by a dense forest. She'd seen bears, deer, and even moose since moving in earlier in the summer. Although there were times she'd felt very much alone and cut off from the world, she actually felt comforted being surrounded by so much nature and so little civilization.

On nights like this, however, she wouldn't have minded someone to snuggle with, to talk to.

Her thoughts turned to Matt once again. In the past, she'd called him every day–sometimes two or three times a day. They send a dozen or more texts between the two of them. She'd almost always fallen asleep shortly after their nighttime chat, reassured by the idea that even though he was geographically far away, his voice could be right there in the room with her. He'd understood her better than anyone, even better than Andrew. He'd loved her unconditionally–all her quirks, nuances, and character traits that had turned others off. And he was loyal to a fault. Matt had always been right there by her side, whether she'd needed him or not.

"Everyone is going to say you're crazy," Taryn whispered to herself now. "People spend their whole lives looking for someone like him and here you go, just throwing him away."

Once she'd started, though, she'd had to go through with it. Kelly Willis had been singing "Sincerely" on her radio while she had that last conversation with him and the irony had not been lost on Taryn. As the alt-country queen had apologized to her lover for letting him down and not having the heart to stay, Taryn had clutched her cell phone and tried to find the right words to gently break her best friend's heart.

To him she'd said, "Your next girlfriend is going to be calling me, thanking her lucky stars that I was such a moron to let you go."

So why? *Why* had she done it?

Taryn closed her eyes and brought the comforter closer. She'd done it because, at heart, she was a closeted romantic. And she just hadn't been in love with him.

Taryn was mature enough to know that love came in different forms and that the love in movies and romance novels was mostly unrealistic. She knew that the bells and whistles most people felt in the beginning were simply hormones and that the lightning bolts faded eventually for everyone. In the end, friendship was probably the most important part of any relationship.

All those things *should* have made her stay with Matt. And, had Miss Dixie not started revealing *her* secrets, she probably would have stayed with him. However, Taryn had peeked behind a curtain and seen something that most would never see and an almost magical world of unlimited possibilities had been revealed. She'd learned to trust her gut and to believe in things that she hadn't previously thought possible.

And she believed there was something else out there for her.

There was absolutely nothing logical about the hunch, it was purely based on intuition. Taryn knew that the likelihood of meeting another man was not great. Unless she picked someone up at the movie theater or in the doctors' office, she was probably not going to connect with anyone any time soon.

And time was *not* on her side.

Still, she could not shake the nagging feeling that she'd made the right decision–even when her mind told her she was nuts.

The mournful waltz had her unexpectedly upright, her eyes darting wildly around the room. At first, she thought it was coming from her television. They were in the diner, however, drinking coffee and there was no music in the scene. Taryn shook her head, cleared her mind, and fell back down on the bed.

When the somber melody struck again, though, she grabbed for the remote and "muted" the sound. Even though the wind continued to wail and moan, making it unnecessarily difficult to hear anything inside the walls, Taryn held her breath and focused intently on the sounds of the house.

The three-time music echoed below her, gently rising and falling in time with her heartbeat. She swallowed hard and slowly slid off the bed. Standing now, she could feel the vibrations of the music reverberating through the floor. Taryn tiptoed to the bedroom door. It faintly creaked as she nudged it open with her big toe; the boards beneath her groaned in protest with each step.

Now, standing on the second-floor landing, she could hear the notes more clearly. They were coming from the parlor right below her. The music fought against the rumbles of thunder and wailing moans of the wind but she recognized an old-fashioned tune her grandmother had enjoyed. For a moment, Taryn thought she saw a glimmer of light at the foot of the stairs, perhaps the glow of a lantern, but then it was gone.

It might have been her imagination.

She wanted to go down and find the source of the music. In the past, she would have called Matt and kept him on the phone with her as she did so. But even though they were still friends, that was no longer her right; she'd given up that right when she'd given up on him.

Now, Taryn leaned against the railing and closed her eyes as she listened until the notes drifted off and the house was filled with nothing more than the echoes of the storm again.

It was a piano that had been playing the delicate waltz. Her father had played the piano at times and she'd recognized the sounds of the keys.

Taryn turned and let herself back into her bedroom, shutting the door firmly behind her and latching it, though that did little to settle her.

Sarah's house didn't have a piano.

THREE

Sara's House, RPH (Cooper House, Lexington, Kentucky)

Taryn *had spent the morning polishing* all the silver in the china cabinet. Charaty would have done it for her, even enjoyed it if Taryn was reading her right, but she wanted something to do. Without a job to go to or a project to work on, Taryn was at a loss. A friend of hers had set up a gallery showing at a Nashville arts center and she'd tried spending the morning working on her photographs, but she'd ended up depressed. Each picture she studied was a reminder of what she could no longer do. Taryn didn't normally indulge in self-pity but just looking at all the old houses and locations she'd once enjoyed working at saddened her.

Would she *ever* be able to work again? Would she ever know the joy of driving up to a new location, getting out with Miss Dixie and exploring its nuances? Know the satisfaction of looking at her finished canvas, watching the past come alive through her paintbrush?

Taryn wasn't sure. All she knew was that her legs were aching, she'd vomited three times since seven that morning, and the furthest she was getting from her house was the front porch.

"I'm ready for my dinner party now," she chuckled as she sat back and took in the dozens of pieces of silverware shining in the rays of sunlight that flooded through the window.

The dining room was a beautiful space. She loved the old walnut table, big enough for ten, and matching china cabinet. Taryn could just imagine hosting parties there, watching everyone come in from their wagons and horses in their skirts, petticoats, and top hats. Pushing back the furniture in the parlor after dinner and dancing...

The music.

Taryn rose to her feet now, wincing as her bones cracked under her slight weight. She proceeded stiffly and carefully—too quickly and she'd throw something out of joint. It felt like one of *those* days.

The parlor was next to the dining room and she went there now. The velvet-covered settee and chair faced the fireplace in an inviting arrangement and she settled there now. She was certain that there had been a piano at one time, but not in *her* lifetime. Sarah had filled the room with books and file folders but Taryn had removed most of them; the books were all outdated educational materials from Sarah's time as a school principal. Not only had she kept a resource library at her house, but she'd also kept dutiful notes over the years, all safely tucked away inside color-coded binders. Taryn kept those; occasionally she'd pull one out and look at the spidery handwriting and feel her eyes water.

Before Taryn could get very far in her thoughts, she was interrupted by the rumble of her nurse's little sports car coming up the hill; the sound of flying gravel had her jolting.

By the time she reached the front door to let her in, Bridget was already on the porch, hopping impatiently from one foot to the other. She wasn't bored or antsy–the woman was just a bundle of energy. From what Taryn could see, it never truly stopped. She wished she had such a reserve. Even in her healthy years she'd been a slow mover.

"Hiya!" Bridget called from the other side of the screen.

Taryn smiled and unlatched the door. Her nurse advanced through the rooms with ease and familiarity, she knew her way around, and Taryn stood back while she began setting up in the dining room. With little else to do, Taryn retired to the kitchen where *she* began fixing them a pot of tea.

Taryn was technically under Hospice care, although, as they were quick to point out, that didn't necessarily mean she was dying. When she'd first heard the word "hospice" she imagined checking herself into a comfortable hotel-style room where nurses shot her up with morphine around the clock and waited for her to pass away in her sleep. What she was receiving, however, was palliative care.

Bridget basically came out on a regular basis to monitor the morphine pump they'd installed in Taryn's stomach, counsel her mental health issues, and run her through strengthening exercises. She'd been opposed to the idea at first, thinking it would be easier to just drive into the city a few times a month and get everything done there. Getting out of the house was a *good* thing.

Oh, how wrong she'd been. To Taryn's surprise, the constant driving back and forth to Portsmouth took more out of her than she'd imagined possible. For every day she was out on the road, she had to spend *two* days in bed recovering. The most she could handle these days was a jaunt into Conway and even though that was only a half-hour drive, it hurt. No, Bridget provided a valuable service and one that Taryn was now grateful for.

Besides, she liked the thirty-five-year-old with the black, pixie haircut and big, bright blue eyes. She also liked the fact that Bridget had heard of her disorder. Indeed, her own brother suffered from it. Taryn had met a few people with it, and it was getting more and more attention, but it was nice that her own nurse knew the ins and outs of Ehlers-Danlos Syndrome.

"So," she began as Taryn joined her in the dining room, a tray of tea balanced carefully in her arms. "How ya been?"

"A little stiff today but mostly fine," Taryn replied. She sat down at the table and Bridget began working on her vitals. "Probably because I didn't sleep too well last night."

"Oh yeah?" She paused with the stethoscope held high in the air. "Sick or...?"

"The storm," Taryn replied. "It kept me up."

"Hmm," she said. With one deft move, she had the thermometer in Taryn's mouth and the blood pressure cuff wrapped around her arm. "We didn't get anything over in Lewisboro. But I'm a sound sleeper so I probably wouldn't have woken up anyway."

"I've never been a great sleeper," Taryn said. "Never cared for the dark."

"You need a husband," Bridget proclaimed.

"A *what*?" Taryn laughed.

"One of those big body pillows that you can stick in the bed with you to snuggle up with," she grinned. "Unless you want a real man. I might be able to help you out with one of those, too."

Taryn snorted. "I think I'd rather have the pillow."

"I hear you, girlfriend."

Taryn waited patiently while the nurse busied herself setting out vials of medication and sanitizing wipes on the table. "Hey, have you ever heard any ghost stories about this place?"

Taryn had learned to become more comfortable with paranormal talks over the years. It certainly wasn't a topic she would've dived right into in her younger years.

"A few stories," Bridget replied, "but I don't really believe in that stuff."

"You don't?" Taryn wasn't sure why, but she was surprised. With the nurse's fantasy-inspired tattoos peeking out from her shirtsleeves, the tiny nose ring, and the small pentagram hanging around her neck she pegged Bridget as a believer for sure.

"I think there's almost always a reasonable explanation for what people think of as hauntings," she shrugged. "We don't know how the brain works, not really, and it could be that in the future the ghost stuff will be perfectly rationalized by science."

Taryn agreed with her to an extent, she *did* think that a lot of times people were just too quick to blame things on the paranormal, but she'd also seen and heard enough in her time to know that there *was* something else out there.

Like the piano music from the night before.

"So just humor me for a minute and pretend you *do* believe," Taryn said.

Bridget stood and started directing Taryn in the stretching exercises that were meant to help support her joints. "What stories do you know?"

31

"Well," Bridget began. "There's the one about the lake and all the caves. With the buried treasure? I'm sure you've heard that one."

"Yep, that one I do. You think there's any truth to it?"

Bridget snorted. "Even if there were they'd have to drain the whole dang thing to find it. My brothers and their friends used to go out on their canoes when they were kids and look for it. They mostly just floated around and cut up, though."

Taryn smiled. She remembered the adventures she and Matt had gone on as kids–riding their bikes around their neighborhoods, pretending bad guys were chasing them. Staying out late to catch lightning bugs in jar, bringing them into their bedrooms at night to use as flashlights. They'd also tried looking for treasure, but all it had resulted in was a very big hole in Taryn's back yard. Her mother had not been amused.

She had a pang then, just remembering the little boy with shaggy dark hair who had once been her closest friend.

"Anything else?" Taryn asked, shaking off the memories. She sure didn't want to break down right in front of her nurse. They were already trying to push antidepressants on her.

"Well, there's the one about the cellar here."

Taryn's curiosity piqued. "Cellar? I don't know that one."

Bridget nodded. "So apparently a long time ago the man who lived here, the one who built the house, he had a daughter. I think his wife died in childbirth or something like that not long after the little girl was born."

Taryn nodded encouragement.

"So I guess there was something wrong with the little girl. She didn't go to school around here or anything. Nobody ever really saw her out in town. Some said she was blind, others said she was mentally impaired."

Taryn could just imagine some of the things that would've been said a couple hundred years ago. It was surprising she'd even kept on living there and hadn't been sent to an asylum, if there really *was* something wrong with her. The rich back then subscribed to the old "out of sight, out of mind" mentality.

"She died, didn't she?" Taryn asked.

"When she was about twelve, I think. In the house fire," Bridget said. "But some people think that before she died in the fire, she went crazy. They think her father locked her up in the cellar and that's why she burned to death. There's a dirt cellar here, right?"

Taryn said there was.

33

"Yeah, well, it has this little rise in the middle of it. Supposedly," Bridget blushed now and Taryn couldn't help but grin, "*supposedly* if you went down there during that time you'd find her sitting on the rise. People said that she 'sits in the chair and stares.' Even after she died, kids got dared to come up here, sneak into the cellar, and try to see her."

"'She sits in the chair and stares,'" Taryn repeated. Her arms were outstretched over her head and she paused now, rolling the words around her mouth. "Sits in the chair and stares. Man, that's kind of creepy."

Bridget visibly shuddered and brought Taryn's arms back to her sides. "It is, isn't it? True or not, I just can't get that image out of mind. A little girl, sitting in a wooden chair on the little hill in the cellar, sunlight streaming through those tiny windows, and her just staring blankly off into the corner."

Now it was Taryn's turn to shudder.

"I don't know," Bridget shrugged. "My guess is that she was just an ordinary little girl that had some health issues and she passed away peacefully here at the house. By all accounts her father was a well-adjusted, honorable man and the people in town respected him. So, who knows?"

But Taryn wasn't so confident. She'd seen enough over the years to know that most stories had at least a tiny nugget of truth.

If there was one thing for sure, however, it was that she wouldn't be making a trip to the cellar any time soon.

*   *   *

IT WAS ANOTHER STORMY, WINDY NIGHT. Taryn wished that some of that rain would soak into the ground; the earth was dry, the grass brittle.

Taryn huddled under her blankets, waiting for the warmth of the fire she'd built to kick in and make her nice and toasty. Sarah hadn't even had electricity for the last few years she'd lived in the house; she'd gotten by on her wood stoves. Taryn needed her creature comforts though. IN addition to central heat and air, there were three working fireplaces in her new home and she loved them all. She'd need to have more wood delivered, however, if she wanted to make it through the winter. She'd been indulgent over the summer, taking advantage the novelty of having a fireplace to build fires much more frequently than were needed.

The tree limbs lashed against her window with a scraping that sounded as though the devil himself were doing it. Behind the white, lacy curtains their shadows appeared as skeletal arms. Taryn shivered then immediately chastised herself.

"You need to get that damn urban legend out of your head," she scolded herself aloud. For a moment, however, she allowed herself to imagine the young girl sitting in the chair in the cellar, her blank eyes unfocused towards the corner.

The branch slapped the window again and Taryn jumped.

Because she wouldn't rest until she looked, she hopped out of bed and marched over to the row of windows on the other side of the room.

"It's just a tree," she reminded herself. Behind her, the Gilmore girls chatted about Thanksgiving dinner at ninety miles an hour. The noise was cheerful and Taryn was grateful for it.

She paused when she reached for the curtain, her heart thumping so hard in her chest that she could see it moving through her nightgown. For a fleeting moment she thought of monsters and demons and even knife-wielding maniacs hovering outside in the dark. When she carefully pushed the fabric aside, however, she saw exactly what she expected to see–a skinny maple branch, enthusiastically dancing in the wind.

It *wasn't* raining, however. At least not yet, anyway, but the fog had rolled in, thick and dirty, across the yard. She was still trying to get used to the fog. It came almost every night, climbing sneakily from the lake, and when it was thick like tonight she could barely see past the front porch. Now, as Taryn watched the brittle leaves still clinging to their dancing tree limbs and felt the chill of the growing fog, she found herself feeling lonely and isolated. She could almost imagine that the whole house was cut off from the rest of the world– that she might wake up in the morning and find that she'd been moved to a different part of the world, or to another time.

"I'm getting weird," Taryn muttered, letting the curtain drop back to its side.

One of the first things she'd done was replace the heavy brocade drapes her aunt favored to something light and airy. As someone who didn't care for the dark when she was sleeping, the last thing she needed was curtains to make it worse.

Before returning to bed, Taryn added another log to the fire. Sparks flew and the small leaf still attached to the wood caused thick puffs of smoke to billow up from the grate. Taryn fanned them away and then used the brush to sweep up the ashes. It was a lonely process doing these things by herself, a reminder that once she returned to bed she'd have nobody with whom to share the warmth and glow.

Back under her comforter, Taryn turned up the television and commenced her huddling. With the fire glowing and her favorite show on, it was cozy in her aunt's bedroom. Her mother's old room was across the hall but she rarely went in there. She possessed no sense of sentimentality for it– odd for a woman that fancied the past and was emotional over old-fashioned laundry detergent ads and drive-ins. There was nothing about the house that reminded her of her mother. Part of her *wanted* to explore more, try to get a sense of the woman who had been almost alien to her. The other part...

"I spent enough time with her when I was a kid," Taryn snorted. "I know enough."

With the room warming, the flannel sheets soft against her skin, and the dim light calming, Taryn finally found herself drifting off to sleep. Her mind was dozing, but she was still alert to the room around her, when she heard the scratching.

At first, the sound faded into the background of the room–just another outside noise joining the ménage of night sounds caused by the wind. It was another branch, a trapped leaf fighting against the glass panes.

Taryn snuggled deeper into her comforter and rolled over.

The scratching came harder then, more insistent. She punched at her feather pillow, trying to find a more comfortable spot for her head; the noise grew louder.

Taryn wasn't sure what finally made her open her eyes, what made *that* sound stick out above the rest. When she sat up, however, the fire was dying and the curtains were fluttering inwards. Taryn studied their flimsy shapes with interest, still mostly asleep. The way they billowed back and forth, their sheer fabric delicate and pale, reminded her of a dance.

A draft? She shook her head to clear the sleep from her head. She'd never noticed a draft in there before.

Scratch tap, scratch tap, came the noise again.

The curtain on the far end moved back towards the glass and Taryn saw the shadow of a tree branch. As the material paused, however, the branch slowly grew larger and then smaller again, a rhythmic motion that had Taryn gasping.

She was not looking at a tree; this was a *hand*.

Taryn was on the second floor. Unless someone had climbed the tree, there was no earthly way for anyone to be standing outside her window.

In the dimly lit room, she slowly slid off the bed and tiptoed across the floor, her feet barely making a sound. She held her breath and steadied herself as she walked, now keenly alert to everything going on in the room.

The curtain fluttered again and the shape disappeared. When it flew back, however, it plastered itself against the glass, remaining there as though stuck. She could see the dark outline just on the other side, now unmoving. For an instant Taryn thought she might have imagined the whole thing. She was halfway across the room and almost turned and went back to bed. Suddenly, however, it clenched into a fist and moved towards the glass again.

Knock, knock, knock.

Remembering every bad vampire movie she'd ever seen, Taryn closed her eyes and tried not to scream. She knew she could turn and run down the stairs, go right out the front door and jumped into her car, fly through the fog and get her a hotel room in North Conway for the night.

But something compelled her to go forward.

With a trembling hand, she grasped the delicate fabric and pushed it aside with care. There was nothing there–no tree branch, no trapped leaf, no visiting bat or other nocturnal visitor. Outside, the fog continued to inch closer and closer to the house, now impenetrable.

Taryn stood before the window, one hand balanced on the window sill and the other still holding onto the curtain. She wasn't sure whether to feel foolish or relieved. She was starting to move back and drop the curtain when the warm breath filled her face. It was sweet smelling and youthful. There was something innocent about the scent, a mixture of strawberries and sleepiness. Taryn closed her eyes and inhaled, too enchanted to even be scared. When she opened them, a small set of handprints appeared in the foggy glass before her. They remained for just an instant and then, as quickly as they'd appeared, they slowly faded away as though they'd never been there at all.

FOUR

Sara's House, RPH (Cooper House, Lexington, KY)

Strolling *across the yard* in the harsh, cool sunshine Taryn

tried to brush off the feeling that someone was watching her.

As a child, though she'd loved visiting her aunt and
staying in the old farm house, on more than one occasion
she'd had the feeling that somebody was right behind her,
just inches away, scrutinizing her every move. She'd never

seen or heard anyone, but the feeling alone had been unsettling. Since she'd been back in New Hampshire, however, things had been fine. Other than a few moments here and there when she was sure she'd just spooked herself, nothing had happened.

And then the music. Taryn was certain the music meant something.

Now, as she made her way to the small family cemetery behind the old barn, she thought about Bridget's story and found herself glancing over her shoulder every few minutes.

As a teen, Taryn remembered talking to Sarah on the phone and asking her why she'd continued to stay in the old house by herself, even after she'd retired. Why she hadn't come down to Nashville to be closer to Stella, Sarah's mother and Taryn's grandmother. Or even her own sister, Taryn's mother. Taryn certainly understood the desire to stay in her own home, and Sarah's house was certainly something special, but she thought it must have been lonely for her at times.

Taryn paused now and looked around the farm. The old barn was caved in on one side; it hadn't been used in Taryn's lifetime. The trees that surrounded the property cut it off from the rest of the world. Now, in the late afternoon sunlight, their shadows made them look foreboding, as though they were thick with secrets. The Federal style stone house rose high on the knoll, a sprawling thing that stood regal against the wind, rain, and sunshine over the years. Taryn tried to imagine it in its former state, even larger than it was now. The other wing reaching out behind it, forming a "T" to the front. She saw the farm hands rushing around, busy and loud with their work. Cattle grazing in the fields behind the barn. Sheep roaming the cleared-off hillside. Horses taking in everything with judgement.

She wished she could have seen it *alive* back then.

She also imagined her aunt running around the yard, her own red hair flying behind her. Tried to envision Sarah as a little girl with pigtails and freckles. Stella sitting on the front porch with her corn husks and slices of apples drying in the sun.

Funny, Taryn thought to herself now, *that it's Aunt Sarah I feel here at this house and not Mother.*

She remembered that conversation with Sarah about the house again.

"Mother left it to me because my sister didn't want it," Sarah had confided in her. "She said, 'You're the only one who cares about this creaky old place. It will be yours one day and you'll have to take care of it.' Of course, back then I just wanted to go to Boston to college. I didn't want to have anything to do with hanging around here. Things change, of course."

"But you love it now," Taryn had prompted her. Taryn couldn't imagine not loving it there. She had wanted to live there herself. "You take care of it like a child."

Taryn had felt a tinge of jealousy from her own words. It was silly to be jealous of a *house*, but she loved her aunt so much. A big part of her was glad that she hadn't had any children; Taryn wanted all her attention to herself.

"I do," Sarah agreed. "I take care of it and..."

Her voice had trailed off then.

"And what?"

"And everything that goes with it," Sarah had mumbled at last, her voice dropping to a whisper.

"'And everything that goes with it,'" Taryn repeated now, almost hearing her aunt's voice ring out through the lawn.

Now, continuing with her walk, Taryn wondered what her aunt had meant. The house held secrets, she supposed. Most did. Taryn believed old homes had memories and energy, just as people do. Perhaps Sarah, and even her grandmother, had known something about the house that they'd kept to themselves over the years. Perhaps Taryn was at the start of something new.

"Better the start of something than the *end*," Taryn chirped. Off in the distance, a bird let out a lonesome cry in agreement.

The small family cemetery lay beyond a wrought iron fence. It was overgrown with weeds. A birch grew tall from the center of one of the graves. Taryn hoped that person liked trees. She opened the rusted gate now and let herself inside.

None of Taryn's family members were buried inside the small graveyard. Her grandparents on her mother's side were both buried in Franklin next to her parents. She'd never known her father's family. Sarah had been cremated. No, the graves here went back much further than her own family.

As Taryn respectfully shuffled between the graves, she peered at the old crumbling headstones, trying to make out dates and names. She'd always loved visiting graveyards, had found them peaceful and good places to do some thinking. Sarah and Taryn had often walked up to this one when Taryn visited. She had picked wild flowers along the way, weeds really but Taryn hadn't known the difference, and placed them on the little girl's grave.

Taryn stopped now in front of a small headstone and gazed down upon it. "Delilah Alderman," she read aloud. "Beloved daughter. The angels wept."

The elements had discolored the stone over the years and it was getting harder and harder to read the words. Sarah had told her that a lot of people liked going to cemeteries and doing etchings of the stones, but that with time that caused them more damage than good. Taryn hadn't touched a headstone since.

Delilah had been eleven she'd died in the fire. *If* she'd died in the fire, Taryn reminded herself. She wondered how much of Bridget's urban legend was true.

Ironically, Delilah *not* had died in her own bedroom–that room had survived the fire. Had she been in it, she might have lived. Instead, she'd died in the servant's room. Nobody knew why she was in there to start with.

To the right of Delilah's little grave there was a slightly larger one. "Nora Alderman," Taryn read now. "Wife and mother."

Only, sadly enough, Nora had been a mother in name only; she hadn't lived long enough to enjoy her only child.

On past that grave, Taryn wandered to the last stone in the row. This one was smaller, an afterthought. *Julian Alderman.* No inscription, no epitaph. Just his name and dates: 1865-1905. Forty years old.

"Who were you, Julian Alderman?" Taryn asked now. A gust of wind followed her words and rustled through the treetops above her. She felt a chill and pulled her cardigan tightly around her.

Had he been a loving father and husband? A man who had perished in a senseless fire, perhaps while trying to save his daughter? Or had he been a monster, a cruel man who'd locked an innocent child in a drafty, dirty cellar and left her there to burn?

With new sense of purpose, Taryn straightened her shoulders and set her mouth in grim resolve. She needed to find out.

*   *   *

"LOOK, I DON'T WANT TO BE THE WET BLANKET or anything but are you sure you want to get yourself knee-deep in a Scooby Doo adventure? Are you really in the mood to play Nancy Drew?"

"Are you finished with your pop culture clichés?" Taryn shot back.

The person on the other end of the line hooted in appreciation. Taryn didn't have to say much—Bryar Rose was not only one of her most sympathetic friends, but she was also on the psychic side. She and her sister Liza Jane Higginbotham were Kudzu Valley, Kentucky's resident witches. Liza Jane also ran the town's only day spa. People came to them for everything from curses on ex-husbands to massage oils and facials. Taryn had met them on a former project.

"I'm bored, Bryar," she complained.

"Leave her alone!" Taryn could hear Bryar's sister shouting in the background. "If she wants to chase ghosts then let her chase 'em! It's what she does, it's who she is!"

"I wasn't telling her not to," Bryar shot back. "I was just worried that–"

"Give me the damn phone," Liza hissed.

Taryn smiled at their bickering. Like most sisters, they had their ups and downs but, like most sisters, they'd ban together against anyone who tried to drive a wedge between them.

Taryn wished *she* had a sister.

"Bye Bryar Rose!" Taryn called as she heard the phone being yanked away from the young woman's hand.

"Don't listen to her, Taryn," Liza commanded once she'd secured her portion of the conversation. "She's got her panties in a wad because it's not going so well in the recording studio. She's had to pay overtime on her musicians this week and it's got her bitching at all of us."

As an avid music lover, Taryn was fascinated by Bryar's work in the entertainment industry as producer. In another lifetime, one in which she could carry a tune, Taryn liked to think she would have been a singer. Alas, dogs howled when they heard her; she had to be content with turning up her radio and serenading her imaginary audience.

"I heard something the other night," Taryn said. She was sitting on the front porch in one of the old wicker rocking chairs in the sunset, watching the hot pink ball of fire slide down behind the tree line. The white paint was flaking off the rocker, littering the old wooden floorboards with dirty snow. It creaked when she moved but she'd created a soothing rhythm from the sound, one that had almost sent her to sleep. "It was piano music."

"I am assuming there was either nobody there or you don't have a piano," Liza said.

"The latter," Taryn agreed.

"But you've had that house for a long time," Liza said. "Did your aunt ever mention anything about it being haunted?"

"No, not to me," Taryn replied. "But maybe she was afraid of scaring me."

"Why now?"

It was a reasonable question, one that Taryn had been asking herself. "I don't know."

Liza's voice came gentle now, a tender whisper. "Honey, are you sure that it..."

Taryn shut her eyes and gave her chair an energetic kick with her foot. It groaned under the movement, a protest that had the tree frog on the old steps hopping away.

"It's *not* in my head," she replied quietly.

"Okay, you would know. But are you sure that it's," Liza fumbled for her words, "necessary, I guess? I mean, sometimes isn't a ghost just a ghost? It doesn't always have to have a big story attached to it. Sometimes isn't it better to just leave the past alone?"

Taryn sighed. The problem was, Liza Jane was right. She really didn't *have* to make a big deal out of things. She could just leave it alone. People lived with ghosts all the time and didn't do anything about it.

"I need something to do," she said at last. "And the research, the exploring, the figuring things out? I *need* those things right now. If I don't do something, I'll end up just sitting around up here moping."

"Have you heard from Matt?"

"He's emailed and texted a few times," Taryn said. "

"How does he sound?"

Taryn snorted. "Just like a man after a breakup—chipper, without a care in the world."

"Sounds like my ex-husband," Liza laughed, "although I hate to make that comparison. I actually *like* Matt."

"It will be okay. I enjoyed watching the house come back to life again," Taryn admitted. "The new roof, the power washing, the new kitchen and bathrooms...Now that everything has kind of died down, though, and I'm left with the DIY stuff I've kind of faltered. It's the first time in a long time I haven't worked, or haven't needed to."

Taryn's life had been jeopardized on a previous job in a popular tourist community. "For her troubles", she was given a hefty settlement. Though it didn't make her wealthy, it *did* take the edge off the occasional poverty that the self-employed faced. She was living off the settlement now.

"So, what's your camera showing you?"

Taryn was embarrassed to answer her friend. "Er...nothing yet."

"That's different, isn't it? Isn't that the way it usually starts?"

"I, uh, haven't actually taken any pictures of the house since the renovation," Taryn admitted. "So, I don't know if anything is there or not."

Liza Jane let out a slow whistle full of shame. "Well no wonder you're depressed! That good pain medication will only go so far in keeping you happy. You must get back into the swing of things again! At least get out with Miss Dixie and move around some."

She was right, of course.

"Yeah, yeah," Taryn grumbled. "I know. I've been lazy."

"Sick," Liza corrected, "not lazy. But I do think your mental health will improve if you return to something you love, even if it's just on a small scale."

By the time she ended the call, Taryn had found herself promising to work on her photographs and re-bond with Miss Dixie. She really did want to get some new pictures of Sarah's house and it would give her more excuses to go outside.

"Maybe I'll just drop the ghost stuff once I'm doing something productive," Taryn muttered to herself as she started back inside the house.

The scent that met her was overpowering. It reminded her of oil lamps and grills. Coughing violently, Taryn stopped in her tracks and attempted to catch her breath as she frantically searched the room. She couldn't see anything but the waves of heat that were rippling the air. Taryn momentarily feared she'd had a gas leak. She had a second of blind, sheer panic before she remembered the house no longer had gas.

Bringing her shirt up over her nose and mouth and fighting her watery eyes, Taryn advanced slowly through the foyer and living room, taking everything in as she moved towards the back of the house. She passed through the dining room, by the parlor and kitchen, and headed to the back staircase. The farther into the house she went, the stronger the scent and thicker the air grew. Taryn gagged; the acrid taste that filled her mouth made her stomach heave.

When Taryn reached the back staircase, she looked up and hesitated, unsure as to whether she should continue. There were sounds above her, rustling and thumping that could've been anything from creaky pipes to an intruder tossing around her belongings. Her cell phone was heavy in her pocket and she removed it now and pressed 911, ready to push the call button if needed.

Miss Dixie waited patiently on the console table against the wall and at the last second, she turned and grabbed for her, slinging the familiar weight around her neck. Taryn was surprised at how much safer she felt with her camera being there with her. She supposed they'd been through a lot together–her camera was almost certainly her best friend now.

The air was closing in on her and she felt herself go woozy. Fighting to stay upright, Taryn stumbled and fell against the wall. The searing heat that burned her arm and hip sent flares of pain from side to side.

She flinched in response and jumped backwards. "Damn it!" Taryn shrieked.

But now she regarded the wall with curiosity. In school, she'd learned that a hot door or hot wall meant that there was a fire on the other side. Only, there was no "other side" to the wall she currently faced. It was an outside wall; only trees and a field existed beyond it.

Of course, that hadn't *always* been the case. At one time the additional wing had spread outwards and there would've been a door close to where she now stood.

Although she didn't think she'd last much longer in the stench and impenetrable air without ventilation, Taryn reached down and flipped Miss Dixie on. She stepped back and held her camera up to her face and proceeded to shoot a rapid string of pictures.

With each sound of the flash, the air grew denser. She was now barely unable to keep her eyes open. Wheezing and winded, Taryn turned and made for the front door. As she staggered forward, she fumbled for the playback and tried to study the LCD screen through the oily film that covered her eyes.

The scene on her camera before her had her stopping in her tracks. The entire back wall, the one she'd just fallen against, was a barricade of angry flames. She turned and glanced over her shoulder but saw nothing but the blank wall with the pastoral scenes Sarah had framed and hung at random on it. As she lingered and studied her camera, the

55

smell of smoke and oil began to slowly dissipate. The air relaxed around her and her eyes settled on a slight stinging from the throbbing they'd been doing. She could almost feel the flames of the invisible fire gradually extinguishing.

Taryn stood in the middle of the floor and surveyed her surroundings with hesitancy. Part of her felt vindicated–she was meant to be there, to be pressing forward. The other part was still shaken. It had been *way* too real. Taryn had been in a fire once. She almost hadn't made it out. It wasn't an experience she wanted to repeat.

"What do I do *now*?" she asked the room. She wasn't sure what to do first–go outside and regroup, start going through Sarah's things for answers, or get out the Ouija board.

She had taken but a single step forward when she heard the footsteps thundering down the back stairs. The owner of the heavy boots seemingly took them two at a time, running quickly to the bottom at top speed.

This is no ghost–this is a man, Taryn thought wildly.

She turned and began scampering towards her front door, her heart beating in her mouth. As she reached for the knob, however, the deep voice bellowed just a few feet from behind her.

"You're *here*."

Something about the sound, something familiar in the way the man spoke. Taryn was frozen in her tracks. She gulped loudly and slowly rotated, her hand still touching the door. She could hear his labored breaths, smell the combination of sweat and smoke that rose from him, feel his eyes taking her in.

The room was empty.

With unstable hands, she lifted Miss Dixie and, without looking through the viewfinder, took a shot.

When Taryn glanced down at the screen, she fainted.

FIVE

Sara's House, RPH (Cooper House, Lexington, Kentucky)

T*aryn stood outside the house*, Miss Dixie in hand, and surveyed her surroundings. It was an unseasonably warm day and she had worked up a sweat just taking a slow trip around the house. Now, her gypsy skirt clung to her bare legs in damp clumps. She was glad for the tank top, though her shoulders were starting to turn pink from the sun. She had her hair pulled up in a bun but a few pieces had escaped and were sticking to the back of her neck. Still, the warm sunshine was good for her. She was surprised at how much better she felt standing out in it, amazed at how much the fog and cold had been negatively affecting her mood.

"Maybe I should move back down to St. Simon's Island," Taryn said as she looked down at Miss Dixie. "Would you like that?"

A flash of light from her bedroom window caught her eye and she looked up, expecting to see something or someone standing there. The window was empty, however; the curtains were motionless.

Taryn had taken only a handful of pictures since moving to New Hampshire, and almost all of them had been in town or on one of her drives through the mountains. If she were perfectly honest with herself, she'd been afraid to take pictures of the house, not afraid of what she might see but afraid of what she might *not*.

The ironic thing about her ability to see the past was that she couldn't see *her* past. So far, she'd only been able to make strong connections with strangers. She'd seen things from the nineteenth century and from five years before, but very little of what she'd seen through her pictures had been personal.

Taryn thought she'd give almost anything to see her grandmother, her aunt, or even her parents. Andrew. How much she wanted to aim Miss Dixie at the house and bring her back to reveal her aunt standing at the front door, motioning her inside! Or to see her grandmother sitting in the parlor, a quilt on her lap. But it didn't work that way. Taryn had little to no control over what she saw.

Of course, she'd taken pictures of the house in the past. Nothing had shown up then and there was always the chance that nothing would show up in the future. Yet Taryn couldn't ignore what she'd seen the day before.

The man.

Taryn trembled now, just thinking about him. It wasn't just that he was standing a few feet from her, his dark hair mussed and his face pained with something indefinable–it was that he was looking straight at *her*. The furnishings around him were modern; Taryn was not seeing a scene from the past. She wasn't watching the house come alive back into its former glory.

No, he was in *her* time. And he saw her.

When she'd come to on the floor, Charaty had been kneeling over her, her face stern with concentration. She'd been holding a cold wash rag on her forehead and mumbling something under her breath. Once Taryn could stand, she'd helped her to the sofa in the living room and had then mother-henned her in her no-nonsense way, bringing her a cup of tea and some slices of toast with butter.

"Too thin, you are," Charaty had grumbled. "Just skin and bones."

Taryn had let her fuss but hadn't told her anything about what had happened. The house was fine by the time her housekeeper arrived and if there was anything lingering, she hadn't noticed.

Now Taryn reexamined the picture she'd taken. The man was not a *bad*-looking one, but his intensity was menacing. It was clear he wanted something from her. Taryn shuddered again. All those times of feeling like someone was watching. The sounds she occasionally heard in the house. Had that been him?

Taryn's experience with intelligent spirits was limited. She had mostly dealt with scenes from the past, things that were essentially memories of what had once happened. The few entities she'd communicated with had not always been in the most pleasant sense.

She needed to find out what he wanted.

Taryn loved her camera. Back when she painted, Miss Dixie acted as her second set of eyes. She'd always spent the first few days walking around, taking pictures of the structure that she'd eventually paint. She'd let her camera focus on the details, the little unique features that made the place special. The photos were always for her and though she derived enjoyment from painting, she found the most pleasure in taking her photos. When she was stressed or bored she'd spend hours sitting on her sofa, or her motel bed in whatever town she was working in, editing the pictures she'd so painstakingly taken.

Now, as she brought Miss Dixie before her and began clicking, she felt herself starting to come alive again.

"Are you sure you'll be okay living up there on your own?" Matt had asked of her. "You don't always do well by yourself."

She'd wanted to snap something mean to him, but she didn't. The truth was, in many ways she'd been alone most of her life. Her parents hadn't wanted her. They'd been more than just distant and cold–they were disinterested. Her grandmother had died far too soon. Over the years her relationship with her aunt had tapered off and she still wasn't sure why. And Andrew...

There were days when she could think of Andrew almost in passing, with nothing more than fond memories and a smile. There were other days that the mere mention of his name threatened to drown her.

Click, click.

She slowly made her way around the house for the second time that day, carefully shooting every window, every angle, every graceful slant of the pitched roof. She zoomed in on crumbling bricks with cracked ivory paint, the three chimneys that remained, on the fenced balustrade on the roof. The Neo-Classical style of the old Federal house was simple and clean, even in its elegant grandness. Her grandmother had ordered the front porch to be expanded along the front of the house, southern style, or so Taryn had heard. That was the most elaborate embellishment on the house. Even the three front-facing gables were lined up symmetrically, straight as a ruler.

When she reached the porch, Taryn paused. She carefully contemplated the white wicker rocking chairs facing the lake, the scrubbed pine boards on the floor, the center door with its sidelights and the fanlight above the door. Now of day, the light would be streaming through the simple ornamentation, providing streaks of elliptical lights on the floor inside.

The house came to a straight stop in the back. Still, if you didn't know that there had once been another section, you wouldn't be able to tell. Luckily, a storm the night of the fire had saved the house from total destruction and the new buyers had the money for restoration. Later, her grandparents had also invested in the house.

Taryn turned and took a few shots of the two-mile-long driveway. She could only see the tip of it now; the rest snaked around the hillside and buried itself in the foliage. She was glad that her grandparents had saved the portico. Even now, if she closed her eyes, she could imagine a line of horse-drawn carriages coming up the dirt road, ladies dressed in their finery for music and dancing on the lawn or in the house.

Taryn sighed and let herself give in to her daily wish: to return to the past. She was born in the wrong time period, she just knew it.

The town was first settled in the late eighteenth century by the Aldermans. The Aldermans were from a line of both soldiers and merchants. They later became lumber barons. In those days, the family home had been in town. It wasn't until Julian married that he had the new construction built in the woods. With five-hundred acres, he had plenty of room to spread out. Julian had owned the local grist mill and saw mill, as well as a carriage factory. He'd done well for himself, which had enabled him to live pretty much however he pleased.

The Ossipee Mountains rose around the house to the north; to the south, one of the two lakes formed a natural barrier. Taryn had heard that the local area had once been favored by the Algonquians, that they had settled there and even fought with the Mohawks over the picturesque location that provided good farm land and ample wildlife even today.

Taryn had found bear scat within feet of her front porch, although the closest she'd come to the bear was seeing it clumsily stumble off into the woods when she sometimes drove home from town in the later afternoon.

She'd taken nearly four dozen pictures by the time she encircled the house. When she let herself back inside she was warm, tired, and happy. She couldn't wait to sit down at her computer and start going through the day's work.

First, however, Taryn made for the parlor and began scouring her aunt's bookshelves. She'd gone through all her notebooks when she'd first moved in, but it was possible she'd missed something. There were dozens of them, however, and Sarah's handwriting had been tiny. It would take forever for her to go through all of them.

"I need to make a plan," she grumbled to herself. Taryn didn't mind talking to herself. She rather enjoyed her own conversations.

There was a notebook on the little desk and she pulled out a blank sheet of paper and began jotting down a list of things to do.

"The history of the house," she dictated to herself as she wrote. "I need to learn about the Aldermans and the town."

Taryn had grown up with pictures of her grandfather around Stella's house. The man she'd seen in her foyer was *not* him. She was counting on him being Julian Alderman himself, but it was just as possible that he was a former employee or even a random dude who met his unfortunate demise somewhere on the property. Couldn't rule *that* out.

"So where can I look?" she asked herself. "Okay, the library, newspaper office, and random people in town."

Taryn had discovered that the most knowledgeable folks were usually the general public. She'd found a wealth of local history and stories from mail carriers, restaurant servers, and the occasional man-on-the-street interview.

"Ghost stories and legends," she added underneath that smaller list. "If there's something here then it's been here for a while. I need to know what everyone else knows."

It would have been helpful if she'd had a family member alive and kicking somewhere—a person who had lived in the house themselves and knew something about it. Since that wasn't possible, however, she'd have to go by local gossip.

"Sarah's thoughts," Taryn wrote.

More than anything, she wanted to get to know her aunt better. For years, Taryn's visits had been the highlights of her childhood. She'd thought her aunt had enjoyed them as well. There was a reason why they'd stopped and Taryn needed to know *why*. Had she been too much of a handful? A burden? Had her single, independent aunt no longer enjoyed having rambunctious, chattering young girl following at her heels everywhere she went?

Taryn let her hand drop, the sheet of paper drifting to the floor. She was suddenly hit with a pang of self-pity. Had she not wanted her anymore? "Doesn't *anyone* want me?" Taryn whispered.

Everyone had left her, or given her up. Her parents had more or less given her away to her grandmother. Andrew had left her during an argument, blowing off steam in a car ride from which he'd never return. Her grandmother had suddenly passed away, leaving her alone. Even Matt...he'd given her up so easily. Hadn't even argued when she'd broken things off with him. He'd basically, in his laid-back way, told her that he still cared and to enjoy her life. And Sarah had stopped inviting her to visit.

"Am I really that easy to get rid of?" Taryn was embarrassed by the hoarseness of her voice and the hot tear that slid down her cheek. When she died, would anyone even notice? She could lay there in the house, dead for days, until Charaty or Bridget showed up for their scheduled time and found her.

The laughter that rang through the walls was bitter. The man's voice echoed hollow, as though it were coming from deep inside a well. Taryn jumped and spun on her heels, looking wildly around the room to find the owner of the sound.

"Who's there?" she demanded. "Who *are* you?"

The laughter came again. It was coming from the back staircase. Taryn reached for her phone and clutched it in her fist as she raced from the room.

"I have a gun!" she called. Her eyes were on the front door and she hastily darted through the foyer towards it.

"Nooo..." came the whispered reply.

She stopped moving and looked over her shoulder. The voice had come from right beside her, just inches from her ear. She'd felt the warm breath on her neck. The room was empty, however, and she was alone.

Taryn's breath was ragged as she stood in the middle of the foyer, the sunlight fanning around her bare feet through the small windows above the door.

"Who *are* you?" she asked in a tight voice.

This was no intruder, this was *him*. The man in the picture. She'd been right–he *did* know she was there. He could see her. And she could hear *him*.

Taryn had never before carried on a conversation with a ghost. In another time, she might have found the idea thrilling–scary, but exciting. In her current state, however, she found herself growing angry.

"I didn't invite you here," she said with steel. "This is *my* house and I didn't say you could stay here and watch me. Scare me. So just tell me what you want and we'll go from there."

"No," the man barked in return.

For a second she thought she saw the air ripple in front of her. It was slight, just a small burst that might have been nothing but her eyes watering.

In Taryn's experience, restless spirits generally wanted something. In the past, she'd been able to rectify what many thought of as hopeless situations; she'd solved mysteries and closed chapters on stories that had remained open-ended for years. But the idea of someone invading her personal space, watching her and even mocking her, was uncalled for. She didn't care who he was or what he wanted– Taryn was in no mood to play games.

There was a hiccup, the sound of smothered laughter, and it made Taryn see red. "Fine," she retorted.

Her shoes were by the front door. She slipped them on and then marched back to the parlor, shoving her phone into her back pocket along the way. Her face hot with anger, she stuffed her laptop into its bag, shrugged on a lightweight sweater, and grabbed the keys from the hook on the wall.

She could feel his eyes on her the entire time. She could also feel both contention and amusement in the room. She had time for neither.

When Taryn reached the front door again, she spun around on her heel and took in the empty space before her.

"I'm going out," she barked. "When I get back, you best have either figured out how to communicate with me without pissing me off or you can just go confine yourself to the cellar or attic. I don't have time for this."

As she slammed the door behind her, she heard the laughing again. It boomed through the door and rattled the key in the lock.

*   *   *

TARYN SETTLED INTO THE DARK BOOTH at the small pub on the other side of the lake. Although it was dinnertime, it was almost empty. Now that her anger had simmered down, Taryn was surprised to find that she was shaking.

"Things have been a lot worse," she muttered to herself, embarrassed by her fear.

Considering some of the things she'd been through in the past, what had happened in her house shouldn't have upset her to the degree it had. She just couldn't get past the idea of someone watching her, hearing her when she thought she was speaking to nobody but herself...it was unnerving.

"Can I take your order?" Taryn folded down her laptop and gave her attention the young server standing before her.

"Lobster bisque and some bread, please," Taryn smiled.

"This isn't your usual night," the server grinned. She was probably in her early twenties, if that. She'd waited on Taryn several times in the past and had always been friendly, if not chatty.

"I have a routine?" Taryn asked.

Her server nodded. "You're usually here on Thursday," she replied. "So, you're a day early."

"I had to get out of the house," Taryn sighed.

I stomped out after a fight with my ghost, she added to herself.

When her server left, Taryn reopened her laptop and pulled her photos back up. She hadn't gotten a chance to look at them yet, and she was antsy.

The interior shots were unremarkable. Well, Taryn liked to think that she'd taken some pretty good pictures, but there wasn't anything extraordinary about them. She found herself flipping through shot after shot of ordinary rooms

71

with regular old furniture–the same things she saw every day.

Even still, when she reached one she'd taken of her bedroom, she held her breath and closed her eyes, willing Sarah to be perched on the edge of the bed or standing by the brocade drapes she'd favored. When Taryn opened her eyes and saw her own sheer curtains and colorful comforter, she sighed with disappointment.

Well, it had been worth a shot. She had to face it–she might never connect with her loved ones again. Random angry ghosts that laughed at her and watched her when she slept, sure. By loving aunts and ex-fiancés were apparently too much to ask for.

For several minutes, Taryn mulled over the idea of starting her own blog, a site dedicated to the restoration of the old house. Some people were really into that. Or maybe a podcast about the paranormal. Other people on other websites wrote in about *her* all the time. Shared theories about Miss Dixie and Taryn, posted pictures of her job sites and previous projects. Perhaps she should capitalize on her own abilities and history and start doing things herself.

Taryn shook her head in annoyance. No, she couldn't do that. She didn't know the first thing about putting together a podcast and she'd never have the motivation to keep up something as regular as a blog. Besides, the concept felt kind of sleazy. She wasn't doing anything special, anything she actually *worked* at.

She could see her server rounding the corner and start towards her with a tray laden with food. Taryn's stomach rumbled and her mouth began watering at the sight of the steaming bowl headed towards her. She was just about to close her computer again, when something caught her eye.

Taryn leaned forward until her face was almost touching her screen. Without looking up, she gestured to the other side of the table. "Just, uh, put it over there. Gonna let it cool down," she murmured absently.

She'd always wondered what that other wing had looked like, how the house had appeared when it was whole and complete before the fire. And now she could see it. Taryn had created a career out of showing other people what their beloved homes and historical sites had been in their glory days. She'd recreated stunning structures from yesterday out of virtual piles of rocks in some cases. She'd brought the past alive for hundreds of clients, using her knowledge of history and architecture along with her artistic ability to create renderings so realistic you felt like you could walk right through the front door. Her own life, however, had been off limits.

Until today.

Sarah's house appeared in all its glory, fully complete with the added wing gleaming bright and whole in the full glare of the afternoon sunshine.

"Huh," Taryn smiled with pride. "I'll be damned."

She'd done sketchings of it in the past. She was highly familiar with Federal style houses, knew what to expect. Had envisioned Sarah's house in its entirety in her mind many times over the years. There was nothing architecturally surprising about the two stories that jutted out in the back, or the extra fireplace that rose behind the balustrade. The neat and symmetrical windows with the sun reflecting off their glass and the curtains standing straight and unmoving inside. It was all pretty much exactly how she'd pictured it.

Her delight came from the fact that she no longer *had* to picture it–it was now right in front of her, close enough to touch.

The homemade lobster bisque, thick and creamy, cooled on the other side of the table. Her Coke watered down beside her. A family of five entered the pub and were seated at the table behind her; the children argued shrilly as the parents attempted to settle them down while they snapped blame at one another.

Taryn ignored all of this. Instead, she slowly shifted from one shot to the next, taking in the details of each exterior image of the house, marveling with pride over everything she'd captured.

"Oh, Sarah," Taryn whispered, feeling tears gather in her eyes. If only her aunt could see it now.

The pretty row of colorful flowers that grew on either side of the front door (the porch was missing in Taryn's shots). The stone walkway that led down to the circular driveway. Those stones were no longer there; Taryn wasn't sure what had happened to them. The trees growing close to the house were barely more than saplings in her photos. Today, they reached the roof and beyond. A flag blew from a fixture on the balustrade, reminding her of a crow's nest on a ship.

It was only the pangs of hunger that finally made her regrettably push her laptop aside and reach for her food. She kept the screen up, however, and allowed her eyes to wander to the images as she ate.

"You're looking might pleased with yourself there," her server said when she returned with a refill.

Taryn nodded happily. "I worked today. Some good things happened."

"Well, good for you," she smiled. "So, I take it you're here for awhile then, and not just for the summer?"

"Indefinitely, or so it seems," Taryn agreed. "I'm living in my aunt's house outside of town."

"As you can see, we get sparse on people once the resorts start closing for the winter," her server gestured towards the nearly-empty dining room. "We'll still get a few for the fall foliage but come November you'll mostly have the place to yourself."

"I don't mind that," Taryn said. "I kind of like it."

"Me too," the other woman winked conspiratorially. "Since you're going to be here for a while, I might introduce myself. I'm Lori."

"Taryn," Taryn replied, sticking out her hand. They shook and Taryn was surprised by Lori's hard grip. They didn't seem to fit her soft smile, cherub face, and wisp of blonde hair that fell across her shoulders like corn silk. She looked like something off the top of a Christmas tree, but her hands were strong and callused.

"Are you an artist?" Lori asked, indicating Taryn's screen.

"A painter mostly, but I dabble in photography as well."

Lori studied the image currently taking center spot. It was a side view of the house. "Nice house," she commented. "I like the old ones."

Taryn didn't know if she was from around there or not. Remembering the list she'd started at home, and the things she needed, Taryn opened her mouth but then quickly closed it. She had many questions to ask her, but it looked like she was going to become a frequent dinner guest. She'd save her inquiries and space them out. There were lots of things she wanted to know, and to say, but now she only wanted to return to reveling in her discovery. The rest could wait.

SIX

White Mountains, RPH (New Hampshire)

"*A*re you sure you don't need anything else?" Bridget stood over Taryn and regarded her with concern.

Taryn shrugged and pulled the afghan tighter around her. "I'm okay. I was out all day yesterday, doing more than usual. I always end up paying for it the next day. I'm fine."

"Okay," Bridget said, but she didn't look or sound convinced. "Just let me know if you're having any unusual side effects with the new medicine."

Taryn was glad she'd bought the new sofa for the living room. It wasn't historically accurate for the house, but it was super plush and she could sink right into it. Besides, she wasn't trying to impress anyone. All her living room furniture was comfortable, but Bridget was currently pacing back and forth across her floor, studying her with narrow eyes rather than taking advantage of the easy chairs.

"Define 'unusual.'"

"Most people experience some dizziness, headaches, and nausea," Bridget replied. "Sometimes, however, there are some hallucinatory disturbances. Those might require some adjustment of the dosage."

"What do you mean by 'hallucinatory?'" Taryn asked.

"Visual disturbances, auditory disturbances, etc.," Bridget said. "You know–if you start seeing things that you know can't really be there or hearing things that don't make sense then the doctor might have you on too much."

Taryn gulped. Was there really the possibility that she was simply reacting to a side effect of her new medication? Wouldn't *that* be something!

"I'm fine," she insisted. "Nothing unusual."

Unless you want to count the invisible man that makes fun of me and the child that leaves handprints on my windows, she added silently.

Bridget leisurely began packing up her equipment. "I'll be on vacation next week and won't be back until the first," she said. "My friend June will be coming out though. You'll like her."

"Okay," Taryn said. She was about to ask Bridget a question about her schedule when there was an unexpected pounding at the front door.

Bridget craned her neck around the corner and glanced at the foyer. "It's a man," she reported. "You expecting anyone?"

"Maybe the mail man with a delivery," Taryn shrugged. "I ordered some books off Amazon."

"I'll get it then," Bridget ordered her as Taryn began to rise from the sofa. "Just stay there."

It was *not* the mail carrier or the UPS man, however, that entered the house. The athletic man with the bald head and red flannel shirt stood six feet tall, had shoulders built like a tree trunk, and stood in her foyer in mud-caked work boots.

Taryn straightened and patted the blanket down around her, making sure her nightgown was covered. "I'm sorry," she said, "may I help you?"

Bridget stood tense and at attention between them, looking ready to spring into action, although what the tiny little woman could actually *do* in a hostile situation Taryn didn't know.

"Sorry to bother you, ma'am," he apologized, "but my name's Larry and I live at the head of the road. I used to do some work for Sarah a long time ago and was wondering if you might have anything for me to do."

"Oh," Taryn faltered as she looked around the living room. Everything was orderly and in its place. "Well, I'm kind of at a standstill at the moment. We just finished all the major renovations."

"I don't mean to pester you at all," he apologized again, "but I work up at the factory and there were some layoffs. I'm really just looking for some extra money until folks start hiring again around here."

"I understand," Taryn smiled gently. "I tell you what, I am *really* going to need some more wood for the winter. I've got some trees at the north end of the property that need to be cut down. I was going to try to get someone to do that for me. If we did it now, then the wood would be seasoned by Christmas. Is that something you could do?"

His eyes seemed to light up his ruddy face and there was a flicker of a smile before he nodded. "Sure can. You mean those oaks at the bottom of the hill?"

"Yeah, they got struck in a storm a few months back," Taryn explained. "They need to come down anyway. They're better than the pine I was using."

"Pine don't always burn so hot," he agreed.

They took a few minutes to settle on a fair price and then he excused himself, promising to return the next day. When he'd let himself out, Bridget surveyed Taryn with concern. "You really want a strange man up here working while you're here alone?"

"As long as he isn't up here at the crack of dawn, then yeah," Taryn replied. "I've had strange men up here working all summer. My house has been a veritable train station."

Taryn's nurse did not look convinced.

"Besides, if he worked for my aunt then I'm sure he's fine," Taryn said with a wave of her hand. "And I do need the wood."

"Just keep your phone close by," Bridget advised her. "I trust *nobody*."

*　　*　　*

TARYN STOOD IN THE YARD AND CONTEMPLATED THE balustrade. From where she stood, the parapet towered above her like a sentinel. It was in bad shape when she'd first moved in, but it hadn't taken her long to get it looking right again. Well, maybe not "her" but she'd supervised. Now, however, the railing had come unhinged and was dangling to one side.

"Musta been the wind last week," Taryn muttered.

She could call someone to come back out, or wait until Larry came over the next day for the wood, but she didn't want it to fall off and shatter in the meantime. Besides, it wasn't like she was totally helpless. Taryn knew her way around a hammer and nails. Andrew had been an architect but he'd also spent his summers in college as a construction worker. He'd taught her stuff.

There was a tiny door in the attic that would take her up on the roof. Taryn stopped in the kitchen on her way and gathered her tool set–pink, of course–and then made her way upstairs. By the time she reached the top of the steep attic stairs, she was huffing and puffing from exhaustion. It was a long way up.

The attic was technically big enough to be its own legitimate room. Sarah had told her that the original owners had actually used it as a ballroom on occasion. She couldn't imagine trying to lug any instruments up there, and it must have been hot in the summertime, but the soaring ceilings, ample space, and beautiful pine floors did kind of beg to be danced upon. The attic spread across the width and length of the entire house. Her old Nashville apartment would have fit into it twice.

Taryn had moved some of Sarah's things into the room. Since she was using a lot of the furniture and accessories herself, there was only a small pile of belongings up against the wall. They were dwarfed in the large room. Taryn took a moment and inspected them with sadness. Sobering to think that a life could come down to a few boxes and suitcases in the corner of your own attic.

Taryn continued to think about this as she pried open the rooftop door and hoisted herself into the air. Who would take care of her things when *she* died? Matt would have at one time. Liza Jane maybe? Her friend Nicki? Nicki was all the way in Wales, but she still loved Taryn. They were still close.

Kind of a lot to ask of Nicki to have to come all the way from the U.K. to pack up my stuff, though, Taryn thought gloomily.

She was pleased to see that the railing wasn't broken, it had only come unattached. With two nails in her mouth, she gripped her pink-handled hammer in her right hand and held firmly to the railing in her left and began pounding. The *whack, whack, whack* was solid and somehow therapeutic.

We don't believe surgery is going to be beneficial for your aneurysm.

Whack.

The best estimate I can give you is $3,000.

Whack.

For parts.

Whack, whack.

I'm not going to try to talk you out of it, Taryn, because I know it's what you want.

Whack.

Sorry ma'am, but it doesn't look like much is going to be salvageable. It's too bad your apartment was on the top floor. The one underneath you barely got touched!

Whack.

It's probably not a good idea for a woman like you, someone not used to living in a big house in the country, to be up here by yourself. I don't think you're up to it.

WHACK!

Now, with sweat running rivers down her cheeks and dirt streaked up her arms, Taryn bounced down the attic stairs two at a time. Feeling accomplished and more than a little pride, she paused on the landing and contemplated the bathroom shower and then decided to head to the kitchen first for a snack.

She'd taken one step down when the gust of wind shot up the staircase and hit her like a ton of bricks. Taryn gasped and stumbled. As she reached for the bannister to steady herself, her canvas tool bag went flying. She watched in horrified amazement as it flew through the air, seemed to hover halfway between the floors, and then crashed to the floor with a resounding thud.

The wind belted around her, pounding her with the gales of a hurricane. She clung to the bannister in terror, her hair flying about her face and blinding her. Tears sprang to her eyes as she cried out and scrambled to keep her balance. The intensity of the outburst had blood rushing to her head, the rhythmic pounding in her ears deafening. The accompanying stench, rotten and pungent, turned her stomach until she thought she might vomit.

"Julian!" Taryn cried. "Why!?"

Then, to her horror, she was lifted completely off her feet. Her legs shot out behind her as she became horizontal with the staircase.

"Julian!" she screamed again.

She'd waxed the bannister just a few days before. Now, she felt her fingers slipping from it. As she struggled to hold on, the terrible smell grew stronger and stronger until she was gagging in revulsion. When one final gust hit her from above, her fingers finally lost their grip. Taryn braced for impact as she flew backwards, her stomach and knees taking the brunt of the blow at the bottom of the stairs.

For a moment, Taryn saw literal stars. As she lay there at the bottom of the stairs and listened to the squall go from a storm to a gentle breeze and then to stillness, she cried.

SEVEN

New Hampshire, RPH

The *miniscule library* consisted of one small room, a smaller community room, and a row of six computers against the back wall. The computers were currently full of middle-aged men and women checking Facebook.

"Hi," Taryn began as she approached the desk. "I just moved here and I'm trying to find some information about the town. General history and more specific history about the house I'm living in."

"Okay," the elderly woman replied. She pushed her thick glasses up on her nose, brushed down her navy skirt, and moved slowly towards the computer. "Where are you living, dear?"

Taryn wasn't sure if the house had an actual "name" or now. "Um, Julian Alderman's house? Big stone house in the woods?"

The other woman paused and considered Taryn over the top of the glasses. "We call it the 'Rock House.'"

"Good to know," Taryn replied cheerfully. "Are there any newspaper articles about the fire, Julian's business dealings, the investigation or anything?"

The woman began typing furiously on the keyboard, her gnarled fingers moving like lightning. "No investigation," she said quickly. "It was storming that night. House caught fire from the lightning and the rain put it out. Not everything is insidious."

Ha, if you only knew the house, Taryn thought in response.

"Well, do you have any microfiche or records here that I could look at?" Taryn tried again.

"Not here," the librarian answered. "You might try the Historical Society, though. They have a small museum in the back."

"What about the local paper?"

"Haven't had one in twenty years. Whole building burned down in the nineties, nothing survived."

"Huh." Well, she guessed it was time to find the Historical Society then. "What time do they close? The Historical Society?"

"They're open once a month, the second Saturday." It was currently Wednesday the first.

Taryn was at a loss. She'd woken up early after a restless night's sleep. She'd been ready and motivated to learn some answers.

"I *do* have some books here that you might be interested in, however," the librarian offered her first smile. "They're in our special collections."

The town's special collections consisted of one row of dusty, leather-bound books. They smelled of mold and some of the pages were so brittle that the threatened to fall from the binding but Taryn was excited to see that at least two of them were histories of the county.

She waited patiently while the librarian carefully collected what she was looking for and carried them over to a small table for Taryn. Then, when she was gone, Taryn quickly pulled out a chair and dove in.

*   *   *

THREE HOURS LATER AND SHE HADN'T FOUND the answers she'd been looking for.

The history of the town went way back, back to the middle of the eighteenth century. She learned about the original Alderman family, about the settling of the town. The Algonquin and Mohawks. Trade and commerce. There was little about Julian Alderman, however, who came later.

The town was originally granted to three young men, including Julian's grandfather, by the Governor of New Hampshire in 1751. The governor had built a summer estate in town near the lake–an estate that no longer stood. The town had subsequently become a kind of summer resort place, frequented by the wealthy and politically minded alike. They came from all over New Hampshire and Maine, as well as from Boston.

For the people who lived there full time, the community relied heavily on agriculture. It lay on a major trade route and provided resources to those both in the north and the south. Its sawmill, owned by the Aldermans, also provided commerce–the wood products and lumber were considered high quality. Eventually, dairy products, wool, and pewter became industries around the county.

Tourism as an industry truly picked up after the Civil War when the railroad was built. Before then, it had been a hub for the wealthy and well connected. Once the lines were put in, middle class citizens were able to travel more efficiently and they began flocking to the site as well. The two lakes that lay on either side of town offered a plethora of water activities and the woods provided ample hunting and outdoor opportunities. Grand resorts, some of which had been turned into summer camps and retreat centers in recent years, were constructed with modern facilities and amenities. Ladies could play lawn games and go for strolls around the lake while the gentlemen hunted and took to the water in sailboats.

Taryn learned of the good times the community had enjoyed, the abundance of wealth and prosper. But she also learned of the sad times that had hit as well.

Crops had a history of dying. Between 1760 and 1930, there were thirty-five years of failure. No discernible cause in any of the cases. Of course, this was a catastrophe for a farming community, and one of the reasons why tourism as a viable industry became pushed.

The town also seemed to have a disproportionate amount of mental illness. At one point the town had more than 1,100 residents. However, the insane asylum in Manchester reported that forty-three of its patients had come from Lewisboro. Zero patients were reported from surrounding communities.

Taryn had come across this tidbit of information from a footnote.

"Not something they probably bragged about in their tourism campaigns," Taryn whispered.

An older woman with tight brown curls and an Army fatigue jacket glared at her from the next table over. She had a stack of paleo cookbooks beside her.

"Sorry," Taryn whispered in return.

The sawmill and gristmill had both been rebuilt half a dozen times because of fires. All the instances were arson related—all from local citizens that possessed no previous criminal record.

The tourists were not immune.

"In 1896," Taryn read quietly, "Janet Overbee of Dover was summering at the Kingswood Resort with her husband, mother, and four children. Mrs. Overbee was an active member of her community and church. She was a member of the Women's Guild and frequently volunteered her time to the children's hospital. By all accounts she was a mild-tempered, compassionate, and well-spoken young woman. Her husband, Mr. John Overbee, was a physician."

Uh oh, Taryn thought to herself, *this is not going to end well.*

One night, after dinner in the resort's main dining room, she quietly put her children to bed. She then returned to the parlor where she slipped poisoning into the cordial glasses of her mother and husband. Once they were incapacitated, she returned to her children's room and proceeded to smother each one in their sleep with their pillows, before turning her husband's revolver on herself.

In 1915, another tourist, this time a man, had open fired in a crowded room during a billiard's match. He injured ten and killed six. Later, the man had no recollection of what had happened.

In one odd statistic, local law enforcement reported that there were more robberies, murders, and domestic disturbances reported in Lewisboro than in any other New Hampshire town of its size. Many of the murders remained unsolved. There was also a high rate of birth defects and infant mortality.

Dang, Taryn thought. *I should have read all of this before I moved here.*

None of this news made her feel very confident.

There were so many reports of crime and mental illness that some believed the local water source was tainted.

"Sticking to bottled from now on," Taryn half-joked aloud. "Even for showers." She certainly didn't need anything new to worry about.

She was about to give it up for the day when she came across a reference to the lake next to her house. Taryn flipped back a page and began to read.

"Daniel Lake," it began, "has perhaps the strangest tale associated with any lake in the state. The name supposedly derives from the man who allegedly shot his entire family and tossed their bodies into the lake one by one. Daniel then hung himself at the edge of his property on a tree that overlooked the water."

Taryn sat back and sighed. Why in the world would anyone name a lake after a guy who did *that*? She knew, of course, that it was probably an urban legend. Daniel was almost certainly someone who lived nearby or helped settle the town. Still...

She shuddered, just thinking of a man grabbing his shot gun and walking around his property searching for his family. She could almost hear the roar of each firing, see him carrying the lifeless bodies to the still, gray water.

There *was* something about that lake, cursed or not.

*　　*　　*

IT WAS LATE AFTERNOON by the time she set out up her long driveway. The lane was already dark with shadows; the sun wasn't able to dip inside the thick trees in most parts. It was always dimly lit, if not altogether dark, regardless of time.

When she pulled up to the house, the fog was beginning to swirl around the house. For the longest time, Taryn sat in her car, hands gripping the steering wheel, and studied the house. After what had happened the day before, part of her didn't *want* to go back inside. She could still smell the pungent odor, still feel the cold wind raging against her body. Her bones still ached from being tossed down the stairs. She was lucky the stairs had broken her fall. Although she'd hit them one by one, if she'd fallen from a distance there would almost certainly be broken bones. As it was, she was in pain but everything was still where it *should* be.

What am I dealing with?

Her thoughts plagued her as she finally left her car and unhurriedly began her ascent to the house. Was it the angry ghost of Julian? Had he gone crazy like the rest of the county and set his own house on fire, killing his daughter in the process? Or was it something else, something *worse*?

"Or am I the one going crazy?" Taryn asked herself as she opened the door and stepped inside.

"Nooo…" came the hollow response.

Taryn jolted and looked around unlit foyer. The pale lamplight from the living room inched its way across the floor but most of the entryway was swathed in black. At the far end, she should she could see the faint ethereal outline of someone or something standing against the wall, but it could just have likely been a shadow.

"Are you real?" she asked hoarsely. "Am I just losing my mind?"

"Not insane," came the sharp response. Taryn jumped again when the voice registered just inches away from her. "I'm hereeee…"

Taryn struggled to catch her breath and collect herself. The house keys rattled in her shaking hands. "You can hear me and see me, can't you?"

"Yessss…"

It sounded as though the owner of the voice was struggling to form his words. The voice was strong, the delivery weak.

"Is this Julian?" She closed her eyes and clenched her fist, waiting for the response.

"Yesss…"

A short burst of warm wind flew into her face and brushed her hair from her eyes. She flinched but didn't move from where she stood.

"Are you trying to hurt me?" she asked waveringly. She wasn't sure she wanted to wait around for the answer to that, but she needed to know.

"No." His voice was steadier now. "Protect me."

Taryn's eyes shot open. "Protect *you*?" She laughed at the irony. "Who's going to protect *me*?"

A low rumbling came from the wall beside her and, as Taryn watched in horrified fascination, the picture that hung in the antique frame wobbled a few times and then crashed to the floor, sending shards of glass flying. One struck her in the ankle, cutting through her jeans. She recoiled from the instantaneous pain.

Her aunt's young face smiled up from the broken frame.

Taryn could feel the fear abruptly replaced with anger.

"Well, you didn't have to do *that*," she snapped.

Trying to avoid the pieces of glass, she made her way across the floor to the picture. Taryn bent down and gently lifted the image with two fingers, careful not to cut herself.

"That was an old frame you know," she complained.

For a moment, she almost forgot who or what she was talking to and only knew her frustration.

"*Taryn.*" The command was sharp and quick.

When she looked up, the man was standing not a foot away. His jet-black hair was alive with flames that grew from his head in a macabre dance. His face might have been handsome but she didn't know; the burning skin was melting right off his bones and sliding down his chest like drops of wax. White smoke rose from his hands and fingertips as he reached out to her.

Taryn howled with fear.

EIGHT

Sara's House, RPH (Cooper House, Lexington, Kentucky)

"**N**o, *our library doesn't* have a lot going for it," Charaty told her. "They keep telling us we're going to get a new one, but they've been saying that for six years so..."

"I learned a few things," Taryn said. She was currently sitting on her sofa, flipping through one of the books she'd checked out and brought home with her. It wasn't from the special collections but was a general book of New Hampshire folklore. She thought it might give her something to look at.

Charaty stepped around her, dusting and sweeping the living room with the speed of a roadrunner. She'd been working nonstop for an hour, only occasionally acknowledging Taryn's presence and speaking to her. She did stop now and gestured towards Taryn's CD player.

"Who's that?"

"John Prine via Nanci Griffith," Taryn answered.

"I've heard you play it before," Charaty nodded. "I like it. Sad but pretty."

"It soothes me," Taryn confessed. "I play it a lot."

It also seems to calm down my ghost, she added silently.

"Hey Charaty," she called out before her housekeeper made for another room. "Do you know anything about the lake down here and who it's named after?"

"Dan Riley," Charaty answered. "The Riley's are an old family. They owned most of the land on the other side. A few of the restaurants are there now."

Taryn had thought as much. "I'd read an urban legend about the name of it. I figured it wasn't true."

"The murders?" Charaty asked. When Taryn nodded, Charaty smiled grimly. "Oh, those are true enough, but they came much later. The lake already had the name by then."

"Geeze," Taryn shivered.

"Not the only murders from there on the lake," Charaty added. "There was a young couple back in the twenties. One lived on the west side, one on the east. Families didn't get along but they were in love. Well, you know. Romeo and Juliet and all."

Taryn smiled. It was an old tale.

"Apparently, they snuck out to meet one another in the middle of the night. Met at the water's edge. The girl's father, however, had caught on to what they were doing and he followed her that night. When he reached their meeting point, he stabbed the boy and killed him. Dragged the girl back to the house and she killed herself a week later."

Taryn shook her head. It reminded her of another story about a young couple back in Kentucky. She'd worked a job at the house where the horrible events had taken place. It was a project, and a house, she'd never forget.

"Some people say you can see their spirits even now," Charaty said. "On certain nights, you're meant to be able to see them sitting at the edge of the lake, their arms around each other. You know, there where the Golden Bridge Chinese Restaurant is now."

Leave it to progress to have no respect for the legends, Taryn thought to herself.

TARYN COULDN'T BREATHE.

She felt the thick, scratchy fabric covering her face but when she went to bat it away, it resisted. She scratched at it again, but it was planted firmly over her face. Panicking, Taryn realized someone was holding it down.

She tried to scream but the sound was muffled against the blanket. With the sensation of being backed into a corner, Taryn lost it. She suddenly found herself kicking with her legs and beating her arms. Bucking wildly, she thrashed around on the bed in an attempt to uncover herself but whoever, or *whatever*, was holding her down seemed to have the strength of an ox.

Taryn groaned something primal, the rage and fear bubbling from her. She could *feel* the weight above her but couldn't tell if it were man, woman, or something else. She continued to fight but slowly felt herself losing consciousness; the more the struggled, the tighter the blanket got. It was pitch black and she could see nothing. The disorientation made it worse, somehow.

Just when she freed her left leg and thought she might gain a foot hold, the pressure came down on her neck. Taryn gasped, unable to catch her breath, and choked. She slowly felt herself being lifted from the bed, her body weightless and the room spinning around her. Then she didn't know anything at all.

NINE

Covered Bridge, RPH (New Hampshire)

*T*aryn *had been up since 3:15 am.* Once she woke, drenched in sweat and panting, she hadn't been able to stay in her bedroom, much less return to sleep.

She was curled up in the corner of the sofa, a stack of Sarah's work binders on the floor at her feet. Dolly Parton sang with Linda Ronstadt and Emmylou Harris on her CD player. Their ethereal harmony filled the empty rooms and brightened the darkness. When Taryn was sad, lonely, or scared she found that she was instantly transported back to a happier, and safer, time with her music.

She needed a lot of that right now.

Taryn had been wrong about Sarah's notebooks. She'd thought that they only contained notes and ideas about her school and administrative work. And while there *was* quite a bit regarding lesson plans, PTA events, and budget problems, in the middle of all that she'd found the personal items as well. Apparently, Sarah had been quite the journalist; she'd just hidden her journals in plain sight.

So far, Taryn had been through three binders. She'd found approximately forty pages on Sarah's thoughts, dreams, and ideas. For the most part, they'd been mundane. Sarah had written a lot about gardening, for one thing— planting season, ideas for rotations, composting tips, etc. She'd keep a detailed log of dates, times, and plants and then measured her crops as they grew. Sarah had also loved her flowers and was fastidious in keeping excellent records in regards to seed storage, pruning, and landscaping ideas. Sarah's gardens were one of Taryn's fondest memories. She could still recall waking up to find her aunt outside in the early morning sun, the big straw hat perched on her head and her white gardening gloves muddy with wet earth. She'd always spend the summer and fall canning; the kitchen had often smelled like sale and boiling water.

Unfortunately, the gardens had all died out in the past few years of Sarah's life. The only remaining remnants were the rusty fences and stone garden creatures, paint faded and chipped from the sun and rain.

She hadn't traveled much but, when she did *get* out of town, she'd favored shows and museums in Boston and New York. She'd had insightful, and sometimes funny, comments about what she saw and did. One entry, dated 2000, read: "Saw 'Swing' last night. After watching two hours of dancing, my feet are hurting for the performers. I won't have to exercise for the week. Felt entirely overdressed in my slacks and blouse. What the hell happened to Broadway?"

On a trip to Boston she'd come back through Salem and stopped for the day. "Went through the House of the Seven Gables," she wrote. "Who knew Nathaniel Hawthorne had been such a stud? Loved the house. I've decided to live there now. Went into a Wiccan shop in the tourist district and asked the salesgirl for the best spell for hexing an annoying co-worker. She looked at me like I had two heads. Nobody takes their job seriously anymore. Whatever happened to customer service?"

She always traveled alone.

Unfortunately, there was very little about the house. She'd occasionally mention the leak in the roof, a power outage, or the need for more firewood but there were no indications that Sarah'd experienced the trouble that was plaguing Taryn.

Still, reading the notebooks made Taryn feel closer to her.

At the end of the sixth one, she reached a page that referred to her own upcoming visit. "I'm looking forward to visiting with my niece," she had written. "I hope I'm not too much of a bore for her. I am sure staying with me in the mountains isn't anywhere near the excitement she has from living in the big city."

Taryn snorted and smiled. As a child, she'd thought nothing was more thrilling than visiting her aunt. Taryn read on, hoping that her aunt would say more and offer insight on her feelings towards her visit, but she didn't. Instead, she began talking about airing out the house and buying new sheets.

Two pages later, however, after notes she'd jotted down following a faculty meeting, Taryn saw something that *did* catch her eye.

"I mustn't let Taryn wander down to the lake alone," she wrote. "Not after what happened to me today."

The music stopped playing and the house was quiet, save for the rhythmic ticking of the grandfather clock. Taryn was now engrossed in her reading, however, and didn't bother to put on a new CD.

Someone tried to kill me today. I don't know who or what it was. I'd simply gone for a walk, like I regularly do, and was standing by the water's edge when something knocked me and pulled me under. For what felt like an eternity I struggled with an unknown assailant. It wasn't until something else appeared that I was finally freed and could leave. As for what that something else was, I do not know. For a moment, I was certain that I saw a man standing in the water with me, a dark-haired gentleman I'd never seen before. He vanished so quickly that I might have been imagining the whole thing. It is possible I am simply going senile and had an episode. Regardless, I don't think I'll be letting my young niece roam as freely as she once did.

The rest of the notebook contained lists of supplies needed for the art and music rooms. Taryn closed the book and leaned back against the cushions.

Was that why her aunt had stopped inviting her to New Hampshire? Had she been afraid for her? Taryn remembered the visit she'd referenced. Sarah had seemed perfectly fine; there was nothing out of the ordinary. Taryn had not felt frightened or unsettled. There had been no indication that anything as harrowing as Sarah's attempted drowning had occurred just days before her arrival.

*   *   *

"YOU SURE YOU DON'T NEED ANYTHING ELSE?"

Larry stood before her, his face red and sweaty from the exertion. A chord of wood was stacked neatly behind her. Two more were in the wood shed in the back.

"I think that will get me through the winter," she chuckled.

He grinned and his face reddened even more. "Well, you don't have to pay me for that last one," he said. "I just didn't want you to get caught up here cold. Power goes out sometimes and you know your drive isn't gonna get plowed this winter. Plows don't go up any further than my own house and sometimes they don't make it that far."

"I'm kind of expecting to get snowed in," she admitted as she handed him a wad of cash.

Without glancing at it, he stuffed it in his jacket. In the flash of the second that she saw his hands, Taryn noticed that were scratched and bruised. She suddenly had a flashback to the night before, waking up and struggling against an unseen assailant. Then she remembered Sarah's near-drowning in the pond. Taryn's heart skipped a beat before she chastised herself. The man had just spent two days that week cutting wood for her—of *course* his hands were going to be a little rough.

"Larry, you ever see anyone wandering around up here that shouldn't be?" she asked.

He scratched his head and considered her question with worry. "Naw, not lately. Someone bothering you?"

"Not really," she answered quickly, probably *too* quickly. "I just wondered what the likelihood of someone finding their way up here without me knowing was."

"Well, there's some hiking trails on the other side of the lake that lead up to that lookout there." He pointed to the cliff on the mountain peak behind her house. Although the peak looked close enough, the distance was deceiving; it was probably a mile away at the least. The drop down was sheer rock. Still, if someone had a mind to, they could definitely find their way around it. But in the dark?

"Sarah never seemed to have any trouble around here though," he added gently. "If that helps."

"Yeah, it does," she said. "I appreciate you coming out here and doing that for me."

"No problem," he shrugged. "Frankly, it's better to have something to do, to keep busy, than to sit around at home."

"I know how that is," she agreed.

Larry thanked her again and then started for his truck. When he got halfway there he turned and considered her again. "Listen, if anyone bothers you, you call me first. Then the police. I'll get here a lot faster."

"I will," she promised.

After he'd driven off she turned and looked at the cliff face again. If someone had been there in the middle of the night, then they might still be there. Hiding in the woods, maybe? There were several hundred acres around her. They could be anywhere.

Taryn shuddered and wrapped her arms around her waist. In the last few months of her life Sarah had bought herself a pistol. She'd mentioned the expense in her journal, but hadn't said why. Taryn wondered how easy it was to use.

*   *   *

THE STORM RAGED AROUND HER, beating wind and rain against the house again. Taryn lay wide awake in bed, the television blaring and a book propped open in her lap. She was trying to distract herself but she couldn't focus.

Every time she turned and looked at the window she saw the small handprints again, even though they had disappeared nearly as quickly as they'd formed.

"Maybe I need to get away," she told the remote as she flipped through the channels, trying to find something to settle on. "Get out for the weekend."

The idea of sitting in the car for a few hours and driving, however, sounded exhausting. She'd gone out to the grocery store earlier and it liked to have worn her out.

When a branch slapped the glass, Taryn jumped. "I'm getting too damn jumpy," she grumbled.

She finally found an old eighties movie and was getting comfortable when the urge to go to the bathroom hit her. "Well, darn it," Taryn sighed. The floor was cold under her feet, even with a fire going, and a draft chilled the bedroom air.

Taryn scuttled across the floor and down the small dark hallway. She could still hear the television, which was comforting, and she willed herself not to think about the child that had perished in that fire so long ago. The fear she must have felt. The horrible death. Had she died from smoke inhalation or been burned? Had she woken up with the smoke thick around her, unable to breathe? Had she awoken to flames burning bright on her bed?

So much for not thinking about it, Taryn thought wryly as she finished up.

She was about to step back into the small hallway when she heard the footsteps on the front stairs. They ascended in a forceful rhythm, heavy work boots worn by someone on a mission. Her phone was in her bedroom, along with her car keys but it was closer than trying to get to the back stairs.

Taryn froze as the steps grew closer and closer. Panicking, she began to violently shake as the image of someone coming at her with a knife or gun ran through her mind. It lasted for a split second and then she took off like lightning, flying out the door and to her bedroom where she slammed the door closed and whimpered.

Despite her fear, she didn't bother to lock it, however. As she'd scrambled past the landing she'd had the opportunity to glance down the stairs and see her intruder head-on.

The stairs had been empty. Whoever was heading towards her was not someone a lock would deter.

Taryn leaned heavily against the door and took deep, ragged breaths. The pounding on the stairs continued and she listened until they reached the top and hesitated. She thought they might go away then, but they didn't. Instead, the intruder turned and slowly began making his own way down the short hallway to her bedroom.

When he was on the other side of her door she held her breath and closed her eyes, willing him not to enter. Taryn moved away and saw the light flicker under the door. Someone was standing there; she could hear their wet, raspy breathing.

"Julian?" she whimpered.

The old-fashioned doorknob slowly began to turn and Taryn moved backwards towards her bed, her hands fumbling behind her for something sharp and heavy. The feeling of total helplessness, of not having anything in which she could defend herself, threatened to overtake her.

With a little shove, the door inched open but whoever was terrorizing her on the other side paused. It didn't open the rest of the way. For a moment, she was caught in dizzying terror and then the door slammed shut, rattling the pictures on the wall. She thought it might be over but then the door once again burst open a couple of inches and then slammed to again. This continued for several seconds, until she thought she might scream.

Finally, she did call out again. "Julian!"

In mid movement, the door stopped in its track. She heard the catch of a breath and then nothing.

Taryn didn't know how to explain it, but tough she knew she wasn't alone, she also knew that whatever had been out there intimidating her was gone.

Although it was useless, she quickly ran across the floor, pushed the door closed, and turned the skeleton key in the lock. She wouldn't be leaving for the rest of the night. She'd pee in her orange juice glass if she needed to.

TEN

Sara's House, RPH (Cooper House, Lexington, Kentucky)

"**Y**ou're looking a little rough there."

Taryn glanced up from her menu and offered a shriveled smile. "I haven't been sleeping much," she said.

"Sick?" Lori asked sympathetically.

"Yeah," Taryn replied, feeling like it was probably the easiest answer.

Once she'd ordered her food, however, and was left alone with her thoughts she began reconsidering everything that had happened. Taryn was certain that what had happened the night before, and the smothering, had been done to intimidate her. She'd felt threatened, not the macabre sense of curiosity she often felt with hauntings. Julian's laughter had angered her, and the sight of his melting face had terrified her, but she hadn't felt intimidated by him in his presence. So why would he try to scare her now? Was she not doing something he thought she *should* be doing?

Taryn knew she was meant to be doing something– she just didn't know *what*. She needed to return to Miss Dixie, to see what else her camera could reveal to her. She'd taken all the pictures of the exterior and had seen the house complete with its original wing. So she knew that whatever was going on involved the house before it had caught on fire. Now she needed to go back through the interior again.

When Lori returned with her meal, Taryn got her attention. "Listen," she began tentatively. "At the risk of sounding totally insane, I want to ask you something."

"Sure, what is it?" Lori's face looked so open and friendly that Taryn barged on despite her nerves.

"I'm currently living at my aunt's house and there have been a lot of weird things going on there. I was just wondering if perhaps *you've* heard any strange stories about it or..."

"There's only one place that I know of that's meant to be haunted," Lori said, "and it's that old stone house on the other side of the lake."

Taryn looked up in surprise. "Well, yeah," she said. "That's it!"

Lori's eyes grew large. "You're living in that house?"

"What do you know about it?"

Lori looked around the dining room, saw that nobody seemed to need anything, and slid into the seat across from Taryn. "Okay, so maybe it's not haunted-haunted in the way that you see on TV, but a lot of really bad things have happened there and around it. And to the people that have worked there."

"Like what?"

"My grandma used to clean the house back in sixties. She worked there for a few weeks and started getting sicker and sicker. Came home and had a heart attack. She was only thirty at the time with no history of heart problems," Lori said, her voice lowered to a whisper.

The two women at the table next to Taryn stopped their conversation and began to listen in.

"She lived, but she was never really the same. My mom said that the guy who died in the fire was actually killed by this man, Ben Warwick, that used to work for him. He wasn't put on trial or anything but everyone knew he did it. Apparently, Ben had been totally fine for years and then just went crazy one day."

This was the first time Taryn had heard that story. From what she'd heard, the house had burned from the lightning.

"Plants have a hard time growing there, the lake almost never has fish, and several people out on the boats have capsized and drowned when they got close to the property," she added.

Taryn was fascinated but continued to listen with a grain of salt. She wasn't so sure about the plants. After all, Sarah had kept detailed records of her garden and things seemed to grow just fine then.

"I mean, most of this happened a long time ago," Lori said with a wave of her hand. "Like in the seventies and stuff."

"She's not wrong." The heavy-set woman closest to Taryn nodded her head emphatically. "Thirty years ago, when I was growing up, we used to go for hikes up around there. Took our dog with us. We'd get within feet of the property boundary and Lucky would start whimpering and wouldn't go near it. Just lay down and cry."

"The hunters say they can never find moose or any kind of wildlife around those parts, even though hardly anybody lives up in there and it's almost all wild," the other woman added.

Taryn was confused. She'd seen plenty of deer and birds. And the bear, too.

"Was your aunt named Sarah?" Lori asked.

Taryn nodded.

"She used to come in here and eat a lot," Lori said. "We all liked her. Didn't know how she could live up there by herself. She was also my sister's principal when she was in school."

Taryn found herself feeling inexplicably close to the younger woman. To know that she was talking to another living soul that had known Sarah in life; it was almost like being close to Sarah herself. Taryn found herself wanting Lori to share every detail she could remember.

"I miss her a lot," Taryn confessed.

"She was an interesting woman," Lori agreed. And then, as though reading Taryn's mind, added, "She'd come in here with a book and sit for hours, reading and talking. Always ordered a big slice of chocolate cake and one to go. Tipped well, too."

Taryn felt her eyes tearing up at the thought of Sarah sitting there with her Agatha Christie, her little glasses

121

perched at the end of her nose, a bowl of clam chowder cooling in front of her.

After Lori left, the other women continued to talk. "We've always thought that there was some Indian stuff going on up there. Something that made the land tainted," the younger of the two explained.

"It's not a place many of us particularly like to be around," the other agreed. "We've always thought there was something fishy."

As they stood to leave, the older woman approached Taryn and placed her hand on her shoulder. "I knew your grandmother. She was a fine woman."

Once they were out of sight, Taryn found herself breaking down.

*　　*　　*

"I can do it, I can do it," Taryn chanted to herself as she climbed the stairs.

She'd left three lights on downstairs. Both lamps in her bedroom and the bathroom light upstairs were on as well. From the outside, it probably looked like she was having a party.

Taryn had considered sleeping on the sofa for a few nights. She had some sleeping tablets that she could take when the pain was bad enough that she couldn't rest. She'd considered taking them and knocking herself out.

"Gotta be brave, though," she reminded herself.

In the past, she would've gotten on the phone with Matt. He'd have talked her through everything. Hell, he would've been on the first plane up to stay with her.

Taryn had learned to become a lot braver without Matt in her life. It was something that both terrified her and filled her with pride.

When she finally reached the landing, she emitted a loud sigh of relief. She'd made it.

She was in her bedroom, nightgown halfway over her head, when the knocking came at the front door. "What the–"

It was midnight and she *never* had visitors.

Taryn crossed over to the window and peeked outside. Her driveway was empty. Whoever was there had come on foot.

She didn't think she'd have to use it, but Taryn had plugged Larry's number into her phone. She brought it up now and dialed it. He answered on the first ring.

"Larry, it's Taryn." She began walking to the landing. Below, the knocking came again. This time it was more insistent. "Listen, I hate to bother you but it's midnight and someone's downstairs, pounding away at my door. I don't see a car."

"I'll be there in five minutes," he promised. "And I'll call the police on the way."

Taryn nodded, though he couldn't see her.

Taking one step at a time, she slowly made her way down the stairs. The house was quiet. When she reached the bottom, she released a sigh of relief thinking that whoever had been there had decided to leave her alone.

Knock, knock, KNOCK.

It was there again, the pounding hard enough to vibrate the walls in the foyer.

There were two thin, vertical windows on either side of the front door and a small rectangular one on the door itself. Taryn had left the porch light on and now, hidden in the shadows of the foyer, she tried to peer through the glass. She couldn't see anyone outside. Feeling braver knowing that Larry was on his way, she tiptoed towards the door.

KNOCK, KNOCK.

Taryn jumped and covered her mouth, muffling her yelp.

She had almost reached the door when the same sound came from behind her.

Knock, knock.

This time, it was coming from the kitchen door at the back of the house. Taryn paused and turned, confused. She didn't know how they could've gotten there so fast. She quickly moved to the front door and peeked out. The porch was empty.

Knock, KNOCK came the insistent pounding on the screen door in the back.

After ensuring the front door was locked, Taryn turned and raced for the kitchen door to check on it. She'd no more than reached the opening from the hall when the front door began banging again.

KNOCK, KNOCK.

Taryn glanced quickly at the back door and then around the corner at the front door again. Clutching her phone, she backed into the foyer, putting herself squarely in the middle of the house.

Knock, knock at the front door.

Seconds later: *knock, knock* at the back.

Taryn slid down the wall and landed on the floor with a thud. Covering her ears, she closed her eyes and began rocking back and forth.

Knock, knock.

KNOCK!

"Leave me alone," she cried. "Just leave me alone!"

"Taryn!"

The gentle rapping at the front was from someone else. Taryn looked up and could see Larry's outline through the windows. "It's me, Larry! You okay in there!"

Taryn jumped to her feet and flew to the door, throwing it open in jubilation. "You got here so fast!" she cried, nearly throwing her arms around his neck.

"I drove as fast as I could," he admitted. He entered the house and took a quick look around. "Police are on their way. You alright?"

But Taryn wasn't. She wasn't sure if she could make it through another night without going out of her mind.

ELEVEN

Whittier Bridge, RPH (New Hampshire)

"**D**o *you want me to come stay with you? I can take care of* you."

The gentle concern in Nicki's voice was out of friendship, not out of condescension.

"Thanks Nicki, but I'll be okay." Taryn hoped her voice sounded stronger to her friend than it did to her own ears.

"If someone's messing with you then you need to get out of there," Nicki told her.

"I ordered an alarm system. They're meant to be here in two days to set it up for me." In the meantime, she'd thought about going to a hotel. Taryn was determined to stay on, however, and try to stick it out. She wanted to be brave, wanted to prove to herself that she could do it. She'd spent the past year battling depression off and on—depression mostly caused by her illness. She'd second-guessed almost every decision she'd made and had even lost herself a few times. Now she needed to be stronger. She needed to move forward.

Moving forward did not mean high-tailing it to a hotel when things got tough.

"Besides, I'm not even sure that an alarm system is going to help in this situation," she confessed.

"You think it's a ghost?"

"Some of it, yes." After some of the things she and Nicki had been through together, she could be totally honest with her. She'd met Nicki, and Nick's fiancé Shawn, at a job in Wales. Nicki was a historical landscaper, Shawn an architect. They'd all been hired to work at a crumbling mansion near the seaside. Although the job had been difficult at times, it had turned out to be one of the best times of her life. She wished she could've stayed but, without a visa, she'd had to return to the United States. She missed Wales and she missed Nicki and Shawn. It was working there and meeting them, however, that had given her the strength to make the necessary changes in her life and to move forward.

Taryn didn't want to backtrack on all of that now and mess things up just because she was frightened. Sarah had survived in the house and so could she.

"Well, it doesn't sound like a very nice ghost," Nicki sniffed.

Taryn chuckled. "No, I guess it doesn't."

"So, what are the pictures like? I am assuming there are crazy-ass pictures like you usually take."

Taryn filled her in on the exterior shots she'd come away with so far. When she was finished, Nicki whistled. "Sounds like it's right up your alley. What about the inside ones? Nothing interesting in them?"

Taryn let herself out the front door and balanced on the porch railing. It was another unseasonably warm day and she was enjoying the bright sky and rays of sunshine. In the daylight, with the beautiful scenery around her, it was difficult to believe that the horrors of the nighttime escapades even existed.

"I haven't really taken any inside yet. Just the one of the man I told you about."

"What?" Nicki sounded shocked. "Why not? By now shouldn't you have burned up a memory card or something?"

Taryn felt her face warm with embarrassment. "Um, well, I haven't been feeling well and—"

"Taryn Magill!" Nicki cried. "You mean to say you've been up there how many months and you haven't even been taking pictures? What have you been doing anyway?"

Lying around, feeling sorry for myself, eating the occasional lonely dinner out in town, snooping around in my dead aunt's stuff, doping myself up on morphine, feeling sorry for myself, Taryn replied soundlessly.

"You know, I was restoring the house, getting my bearings. Organizing Sarah's things. Learning about the area. Stuff," Taryn finished feebly.

Nicki was quiet on the other end. When she spoke at last, her voice was tender. "It's no wonder you've been feeling bad, dear. Your art and music are your life. I know you can't work like you once did but if you're not at least playing around with your pictures and paints, even just for fun, then you're not being *you*."

Liza Jane Higginbotham had told her something similar.

"Hold on, Shawn wants to say something to you."

When Shawn got on the phone, Taryn was surprised at how glad she was to hear his voice. "Hey," he said gently. "How you doing over there?"

"Not so good," Taryn replied. She was mortified to hear her voice cracking. "I'm just so..."

When she began crying she could have died of embarrassment. "I'm sorry. I'm so sorry!"

"Hey," Shawn said. "It's okay. It's alright to cry."

Hearing him speak was like feeling a big set of arms wrapping themselves around her. Taryn wasn't sure she believed in past lives and reincarnation but she *did* believe in multiple soul mates. She thought Shawn and Nicki were two of hers.

"I've just felt so *bad*," Taryn sobbed. "So sick and so lost and so scared. My body's in constant pain, I don't feel like I have anyone anymore—and I know that it's completely my own fault for letting go of Matt but it felt like the right decision at the time. This thing in my house is keeping me away at night and terrorizing me. I don't know what to do."

"You were due a breakdown," Shawn assured her. "Everyone gets to have one."

"One?" Taryn retorted through her tears. "How about one a day? Because that's what I've been doing."

"Hey, who's counting?"

Taryn sniffed. "I'm not usually like this."

131

"I know," he agreed. "Listen, what Nicki said is right. You need to find a way to bring the 'old' you into the current you. I know what the doctors have told you but you're not dead yet. Don't stop living on us, okay?"

"I've been doing some research about the house," she said. "Learning about the history. Trying to piece together what's going on here."

"Well, that's a start!" Shawn's voice was cheerful and Taryn could hear Nicki humming in the background. She felt as though a weight had been lifted, just listening to their sounds of life.

"Nicki and I get some time off in December. We were thinking, if it's okay with you, that we'd come over and maybe spend Christmas with you," he added.

Taryn's heart jumped into her throat. "Oh my goodness, that would be awesome. *Please* do that," she cried. "I would love that so much!"

"Maybe go to Boston while we're there!" Nicki sang in the background. "Stay in a ritzy hotel for a weekend!"

"We could stay for a month if you'll have us," Shawn said. "We'd really like to."

For the rest of the conversation Taryn was floating on cloud nine. When she hung up the phone, however, she felt her heart settle way back down into her stomach. The birds were chirping, the gentle breeze was ruffling her hair, and the sun was warm on her skin but she felt terribly lonely.

Taryn went back inside and walked aimlessly around the house, trying to think of something to do. When she saw Miss Dixie waiting patiently on the coffee table in the living room, she picked her up and studied her. "It's time, old girl. I'm sorry it took me so long."

Her camera seemed to forgive her.

Upstairs, the sound of light footsteps began treading the floor in her bedroom. Taryn looked up and swallowed hard. The prisms on the small chandelier swung gently from the vibrations. It wasn't the same footfalls she'd heard a few nights before–these were much softer.

"Brave," she reminded herself. "Sarah."

Oh, if only it were Sarah up there waiting for me, she thought.

With Miss Dixie in hand, Taryn went over to the CD player and flipped on Nanci Griffith. The otherworldly opening notes of "The Speed of the Sound of Loneliness" filled the room. Taryn smiled disparagingly to herself. Running just to be on the run, like the song said. Was that what she was doing? Was what she'd been doing her entire life? Flitting from one place to the other because she didn't belong anywhere or to anyone? Just because she *could*?

Above her, the pacing stopped. For the moment, at least, she was alone again.

Taryn got to work.

*   *   *

TARYN HAD TRULY NEVER BEEN IN AS MANY STORMS in her life as she'd been through at Sarah's house. Back in Nashville, the spring was usually the stormy season. She didn't know *what* was going on here.

Still, she'd had a profitable day of picture taking and was feeling good about herself, good about moving around and doing something she loved. Shawn and Nicki had been right; she couldn't just sit around on her hiney and feel sorry for herself. She was going to be alive for a very, very long time and even though she no longer had a career, it didn't mean she couldn't work.

Tift Merritt sang softly from the other side of the room and Taryn had built a fire in the living room. The fireplace glowed warm and bright and although the storm raged outside, she was cozy.

She wasn't scared, despite what had happened. For the first time in days, Taryn felt peaceful. Maybe there really was something to the whole mental health and hobby stuff.

She'd kept busy all day and now she was happy and content, not huddled under her covers, jumping at every little sound.

With her laptop balanced on her knees, she sorted through the photos she'd taken that afternoon. Taryn was disappointed to find that the ones in the living room, parlor, kitchen, and other assorted downstairs' rooms were unremarkable. The house photographed beautifully and she was proud to see that was shaping up to be something she could be proud of, but the images were all ordinary.

"You win some, you lose some," Tarn shrugged.

And then she got to the back staircase.

The wall at the foot of the stairs was nearly two feet thick. It was a solid wall, devoid of windows, and there was nothing on the other side. Of course, at one time there'd been a door—a door that led to the other wing before the fire.

That door was there, now, in Taryn's picture.

She quickly enlarged the shot and zoomed in on it. Sure enough, the large opening in the wall showed a small hallway with several other doors leading off it. The doors were open now and she could almost see glimpses of furniture inside them. A colorful runner lay straight and attractive on the wood floors. The staircase was gleaming with wax. Several oil prints hung on the wall, including one of an auburn-haired little girl. She was perched on the edge of a rocking chair, smiling impishly at the artist, her dimples deep and sweet.

"She sits in the chair and stares," Taryn mumbled.

Well, this little girl certainly didn't look scary enough to haunt a cellar. And she didn't look as though anything were wrong with her, either.

The one photo of the back staircase was the anomaly of the downstairs' photos. Though Taryn was excited by what she saw, she also felt disappointment. She might never see what lay beyond those other doors. Her camera showed the past, but only if she were standing in the actual space that she was peering into. In other words, she couldn't take a picture of her living room and see ancient Egypt–she'd have to actually be *in* Egypt. She'd worked it out in her mind a bit and had determined that she and Miss Dixie picked up on leftover energy and memories. Sometimes when she stared at a television screen or a picture hanging on the wall and then closed her eyes, for a moment she could see still the rectangular shape shimmering behind her eyelids. She thought her abilities were somewhere along the lines of that. And, because the other rooms were no longer there and she couldn't stand in them, she would probably not be able to see them.

"I guess I could try standing out in the yard," she said aloud. "See what happens."

She decided she might try that next.

The upstairs images were a different story. As soon as Taryn flipped to the first shot taken at the top of the stairs, she knew she was looking at something special.

The landing was currently bare. She was thinking of putting in a telephone table to break up the open space but at the moment it was empty.

In her picture, however, she saw a long, thin console table. A crystal vase of yellow wildflowers flourished in the sunlight that poured in through the window in the small hallway.

Taryn could feel her heart thumping with excitement.

In present day, the remaining rooms ran off a single hallway. Since she didn't use those rooms, she kept their doors closed. In her picture, however, all the doors were open and a second hallway ran in the opposite direction from the landing. It was this anomaly that she focused on. There were three rooms she'd never seen before but, like the downstairs shot, she could only just get a faint peek of what lay beyond. Taryn had gone inside the rooms that still existed, however, so she moved on to them.

Her mother's old bedroom was a nursery fit for a princess. A beautiful four-poster bed was placed under the window and Taryn could see the swell of the mountains through the dainty curtains. A group of porcelain-faced dolls

137

were lined up on the richly embroidered bedspread. A rocking horse waited patiently in one corner of the room, a tall, Victorian dollhouse in another. A wardrobe against the wall was partly open, displaying an abundance of lacy dresses and little girls' petticoats. On the bureau, she could make out a selection of silky hair ribbons, each one folded daintily. There was also a silver vanity set, a slender pearl necklace in a small, gold dish, and a pile of pinecones. Taryn smiled at the latter. So she might have been spoiled and girly, but she was still like any other child from any other time—she liked bringing in the outdoors.

Taryn felt her heart melting a little for the little girl. Seeing her little things and knowing her fate sent a wave of sadness and pity through her. Taryn was not someone who had ever entertained a lot of motherly longings or instincts but there was something about this child that tugged at her— and she'd never even seen her.

Her own bedroom, Sarah's room, was clearly the master bedroom. A small bookcase by the door held several leather-bound volumes of classics that Taryn was familiar with today. The mahogany bed and matching bureau took up most of the room, with a central table taking up its own fair share of floor space. A stately wardrobe in this bedroom had its doors closed so Taryn couldn't peek inside of it. On a small desk under the window, however, she saw a bottle of ink, several sheets of paper, a small book, and an unopened letter. When Taryn zoomed in on the image she was able to read the writing on the envelope. It was addressed to "Mister Julian Alderman", although the return address was smudged. A washstand held a pitcher and bowl and next to it, on the bureau, she could see a shaving brush and razor. The paintings on the wall were of mountains and horses grazing in fields. Both the bedspread and the curtains were dark green. The only remotely feminine thing in the room was a pink chaise lounge in front of the wardrobe and the delicate white camisole folded neatly over it.

Taryn studied each of these images repeatedly, memorizing every detail. She couldn't contain the thrills that shot through her with every passing second. This *was* her time traveling. It was the closest she'd get to going back to another time. Taryn briefly wondered if what she was seeing in the images *always* existed–if the past and present were existing at the same time. That idea also excited her. If so, then perhaps it meant that her aunt was somehow still there in the house with her. And that maybe one day she'd take a picture and see a glimpse of her from the past.

She could daydream anyhow.

For now, anyway, she had to figure out what it all meant.

She knew that Julian and his daughter had perished in the fire. According to the women at the pub, people suspected his former employee, Benjamin Warwick. She also knew that other tragedies had happened in and around the property as well. She'd recently learned from one of the history books that, weeks before the fire, a local farmer fishing on the property had been strangled to death. His killer had not been found. Julian himself had stopped going into town, no longer socialized with members of the community. He'd all but cut himself and Delilah off from the rest of the world.

"What was going on with you, Julian?" she asked the room. "What were you all doing up here by yourself?"

She received no response. Moments later, the power went out, leaving her with nothing but the firelight.

TWELVE

New Hampshire, RPH

*S*o *far, the longest Taryn had gone without* power in the house was around three hours. She was surprised when it still wasn't back on by the time she went to bed. Still, she had the fire going and could light some of Sarah's old oil lamps so she was fine.

However, when she woke up the next morning, the power was still out. Since her phone had died during the night, she was unable to charge it. Suddenly, Taryn found herself without lights, internet, or phone.

"I'm really roughing it now," she mumbled to herself.

She still had her plans and good intentions for the day, but when she arose to go to the bathroom, her knee twisted under her and she fell to floor. A sudden, sharp pain shot through her hip when she hit the ground and Taryn cried out in pain. She was hopeful to find that she'd merely subluxed it, and not completely dislocated it, but it was still sore.

By the time she hobbled to the bathroom, her whole body was wracked with pain. She spent half an hour by the toilet, vomiting up everything she'd eaten in the past week. Her head throbbed, the blood rushing to her and pulsating in her ears so that she could barely hear herself think. It was difficult to hold her head up. The pain that shot down both arms soon turned to a tingling and it became tough to open and close her hand; her fingers were bright red.

Taryn was *not* having a good morning.

Shaky and dripping with sweat, an hour later Taryn was finally able to crawl back to bed. She had days like this, a lot actually, but she could usually pass them by easily enough while lying in bed and watching bad television. With it out, though, there wasn't much she could do to distract herself. She just fell back asleep.

Sick and pained, her sleep was restless. Taryn tossed and turned for hours, occasionally moaning out and mumbling nonsense. At one point, she opened her eyes and thought for sure she saw someone, her nana maybe, standing at the foot of her bed. The figure appeared to be watching her with concern, but the room was blurry and unfocused and she fell unconscious again almost immediately.

Her dreams were wild.

She was standing inside the house, watching Andrew march out the front door for the last time. Watched as he got halfway to his car and then paused. For a second, he turned around and they made eye contact through the window. He made as though he would start coming back to her. She had a choice then–give him some sort of indication to continue or leave. She walked away. He left.

Taryn woke up sobbing.

Her grandmother waking up that last morning, her body shaking and her face soaked with sweat.

"Do you need me to call the doctor?" Taryn's voice hollow and dull.

"I'm fine," came Stella's muffled replied.

Taryn reached for her but Stella fell away and kept falling back and back until the bed was gone and Taryn could no longer see her.

The teenage girl burning in the fire, her long hair flying around her shoulders and her mouth formed in a perfectly-shaped "oh."

Then Taryn was running, escaping from something dark and malevolent. She saw it, towering high above her and lifeless, closing in on her as her legs turned to Jell-O and the ground to molasses. When its snaky tendrils slithered around her neck, she knew it had been chasing her all her life.

She was suffocating again. The blackness closed in and began to overtake her. Taryn choked and began to sob as she felt the floor beneath her opening. When she felt herself begin to fall through the breach, Taryn screamed.

But then she was falling and the blackness was gone. Taryn braced herself, waiting to wake up. It was like so many of her other falling dreams and now, aware that she was not awake, she was flooded with relief. She closed her eyes and waited for the impact of her bed to meet her.

She hit something hard.

Taryn opened her eyes and looked around. She *was* in a bedroom, but it wasn't hers. When she saw the wardrobe with the open door and lacy dresses peeking out, she knew whose room she'd landed in–Delilah's.

Taryn rose to her feet and walked towards the wardrobe. She was surprised to feel the floor beneath her feet. When she glanced down at herself, she saw the nightgown she'd worn to bed. So she was still *Taryn*, she was just in someone else's reality.

The small dresses that hung inside were both rough and silky under her fingers. Amazed that she could feel them, Taryn's eyes widened. She'd always had realistic dreams, but they'd never been *this* convincing before.

Hearing noises outside, Taryn went over to the window by the bed and looked out. A young girl was sprinting across the lawn, her long hair streaming behind her like flames in a fire. Her face was bright with happiness and laughter. The barn, now upright and sparkling red with fresh paint in the sun, lay behind her. Taryn was filled with wonder; how many times had she awakened in this very house, imagining that she could glance out the window and see the past? And now she *was*.

The girl's yellow dress fluttered in the breeze, whipping around long, calf-like legs. No longer a child, but not quite a young woman, the child was in that awkward stage where she hadn't yet grown into her features but it was easy to see that she'd one day be beautiful.

145

Taryn gasped and backed away from the window, hit with the sudden realization that the girl would never get that chance. Even in her dreamlike state, she began to cry.

"Damn it," she mumbled, reaching up and brushing the tears from her cheek. They were wet against the back of her hand.

She could feel herself starting to waken. She knew she didn't have much time. She was already starting to feel the softness of her bed below her, even while she felt the wood floors at the same time.

Taryn quickly reproached the window. Delilah darted past the window again, but this time she was followed by a man. His dark, curly hair looked coal black in the sun. He was laughing as well, his arms outstretched towards his daughter.

Then, as though sensing someone else's presence, he paused. He looked up at the window and, for just a second, their eyes met. Taryn brought her hand to the glass and leaned forward. He shielded his eyes from the sun to get a better look, his face yielded surprise. Their eyes remained locked for another fraction of a second and then Taryn could feel herself falling backwards.

When she hit the smoothness of her pillow, she opened her eyes. Her television was in its usual place on the other side of the room.

She was probably more disappointed than she'd ever been.

*   *   *

THE POWER STAYED OUT ALL DAY.

"That storm was worse than I thought it was, I guess," Taryn said as she sluggishly made her way down the stairs. She carried a flashlight; the downstairs was pitch black.

She'd spent all day in bed and now she was hungry.

With the power out, there weren't a lot of things she could make. She didn't want to waste everything in the refrigerator so Taryn only had one shot to open it and get out what she needed. She quickly reached for the cheese and deli meat.

With the flashlight balanced on the counter, Taryn made herself a roast beef sandwich with banana and apple slices on the side. If the power wasn't back on in the morning, she'd have to drive into town and find a way to charge her phone and call. She'd just gone grocery shopping a few days before–like hell she was going to let her food go to ruin.

With her plate in one hand and her flashlight in the other, Taryn went to her front door and checked it, ensuring it was locked.

The police had searched the property while they were there but hadn't been able to find anything. There was no sign that anyone had been there. Larry had invited her to stay at his house, claimed his wife was getting a spare bed ready for her, but Taryn had declined. Now she was wondering if she should go down there anyway.

When she peeped outside, however, it was so thick with fog that she couldn't even see her car or the driveway. She could barely see the end of her porch. There was no way she was going to try to drive to the end of the road in it. With her luck, she'd end up flipping down the mountain and they wouldn't find her until spring.

No, Taryn sighed to herself, *I'm better off just staying put.*

Sarah's little pistol was tucked into her nightstand's drawer.

As she started her ascent up the stairs, however, something made her take pause. The house was quiet. She didn't hear a single remarkable thing that gave her cause for concern. Indeed, with the power out the house was *curiously* quiet. It was amazing how much static electronics added to the air. But there were no footsteps, no sounds of another person breathing, nothing to make her think someone hiding in the shadows of her house. Still, she was suddenly overcome with the sense that she wasn't alone.

Taryn climbed the steps with care, the flashlight illuminating the path before her. The bright light made a funnel of sorts; the trail in front of her was well-lit and cheery while the sides faded away into murky oblivion.

When she reached the landing, Taryn stopped and listened. She still couldn't hear anything. There was something about the air, however, that nagged at her. Something had disrupted her, something besides her.

Now, picking up her pace, Taryn darted into her bedroom. It was brighter in there, thanks to the lanterns, and she felt an immediate sense of relief. She walked over to her nightstand, turned, and shined the flashlight around the dark corners of her room. It was clear.

Taryn gave out an audible sigh of relief and replaced the flashlight on the nightstand. She placed her plate of food next to it and tried the lamp again. Still out.

A clean nightgown was folded over the foot of the bed and Taryn changed into it now. Keeping her back to the door, she fluffed her pillows and straightened her blankets. Then, with her stomach gurgling with hunger, she climbed back into bed.

The man that stood just feet away was watching her intently, his expression bemused.

"I didn't scare you," he spoke plainly, his words enunciated clearly. "You needn't accuse me of things I didn't do. It wasn't me."

When he made to step towards her, Taryn screamed.

THIRTEEN

New Hampshire, RPH

*T*aryn had dug out every lantern in Sarah's house—all the candles she could find, too. After what she'd learned on Jekyll Island, she should have known better but she didn't care. The more, the merrier.

Cowered in the middle of her bed with the flames flickering wildly, Taryn surveyed her room. She'd closed the door and now she waited.

"He said he didn't scare me," Taryn reminded herself in a trembling voice. But, of course, he *had*.

As soon as she'd made a noise, he'd disappeared. Taryn had watched it happen right before her eyes. He hadn't faded away or disintegrated into millions of molecules–he'd just been there one second and was gone the next.

Now Taryn chastised herself. This was her chance, wasn't it? Her chance to communicate with something bigger, to have a real piece of the past right there in the room with her. This wasn't a photograph of leftover energy–this was *real*. Did she really want to give in to fear and toss the opportunity away?

No, she didn't.

First, she willed him to return. Taryn closed her eyes, focused on the image of his face, and concentrated as hard as she could.

When she opened her eyes, her room was empty and she felt like she'd been trying to have a bowel movement.

Miss Dixie set on her bureau so Taryn got up, scampered across the room, and brought her camera back. "Maybe *you* can do this," she said.

From her position on the bed, Taryn began snapping pictures, starting on one side and slowly fanning out until she'd made her way to the other. When she was finished, she studied the playback. Nothing there.

"Well," she told Miss Dixie, "maybe it just wasn't meant to be!"

But something in the air flickered then and Taryn sat up straighter. There was a scent in the air, something sharp but not altogether unpleasant. It wasn't anything that had been there before.

"Hello?" she asked. Her voice shook now that things were becoming real again.

The air around the foot of the bed shimmered. There was a ripple, like she'd seen before, and the scent grew stronger.

"Julian?" Taryn whispered.

The man that appeared at the foot of her bed *looked* real enough. He stood tall, Taryn estimated him to be over six feet, and he wore simple gray trousers with a white shirt. His tan face had the slightest sign of stubble. His hair, black and full, was mussed and stuck out from his head in wild curls. His feet were bare. That bemused expression was back again, along with something else. Anger? No, Taryn decided, not quite that. Satisfaction? Maybe. When he moved closer to her, the scent grew stronger. She now recognized it as dirt–like wet mud after a rainstorm. He *could* have been real and yet there was something not quite solid about him. As though he weren't quite three-dimensional.

"Julian?" Taryn asked again. She couldn't quite hold her voice steady.

Ho nodded and then cocked his head to the side. "You know me." It was not a question.

"No," Taryn answered. "But with the process of elimination..."

She expected him to disappear again. She expected to wake up, to find that she'd passed out in the bathroom and the whole episode was a dream. He remained, however, even though he cast no shadow on her walls in the firelight.

"I know you must want something," Taryn said. "But why do you seem to go out of your way to scare me? It seems unnecessary, considering the fact that you're talking to me now. Why the knocking on the door? Trying to suffocate me in my bed? Rattling the knob the other night?"

Julian pursed his lips and shook his head. "I did not do those things. It's rather rude of you to imply that I *did*."

"Well then, who else?" Taryn demanded. She momentarily forgot she was talking to a ghost and only saw him, the man.

"I don't know," he replied. "I can't see."

"You can see me now, though," she pointed out. "Right?"

He nodded. "But only you. I'm not always around."

Taryn reached over on her nightstand and fumbled for her apple juice. She needed something stronger but that would have to do.

"So where do you go when you're not here?" Was she about to discover the secrets of the afterlife after all?

"I don't know," he shrugged. "I have no consciousness when I am not here. I'm around, of course, but it's as though I am sleeping."

"So what brings you out?" she asked.

"You."

His answer took her by surprise. "Me?"

He nodded again and clasped his hands behind his back. "Always."

"You know me?"

"I was sleeping and then one day I awoke," he explained. "Here I was, once again in my home. I knew it was my home but everything looked different."

Taryn opened her mouth to speak and he cut her off. "Yes, I know I'm dead. I was there when it happened."

She closed her mouth again.

"I moved around the house, examined things. And then I saw you. You were a little girl. You slept in the bed next to your aunt. I didn't want to wake you so I remained quiet." He smiled ruefully. "I know what it's like to awaken a sleeping child."

"And after that?" Taryn asked. She couldn't believe what she was hearing.

Julian shrugged. "It came and went. When you were here, I was stronger. There were moments when I awoke with Sarah. She could feel me here, at least I am certain she felt something. Over the years, however, it's been your presence that has brought me here. I know you have questions but I'm afraid I don't know the answers. I can only tell you what I saw."

"A few weeks ago," Taryn spoke now with a steadier voice. "There were hand prints on the window. They weren't big enough to be yours. Your daughter's? Is she here as well?"

Julian's face hardened and he looked down at the floor. "I don't know," he replied at last. "There are times when I can almost feel her, but we've never come face to face."

Taryn decided not to press the matter. "So what do you need of me? To help you get to the other side? I am not sure I know how to do that. I'm not a medium and you know you're dead so..."

Julian raised his palms and shook his head. "I don't know."

"Do you need me to help you figure out how and why you died?"

He laughed harshly. "I died in a fire because someone set it."

Taryn felt herself deflating. *Well damn*, she thought, *I've been barking up the wrong tree. There's no mystery here at all.*

"So it wasn't you?"

He sent her a withering look and she found herself reprimanded.

"I am almost certain it was my man Benjamin," he said. "He'd come here earlier that day, full of anger and threats. I was confused, of course. We'd had a fine working relationship up until a couple of weeks before. He'd changed and I could no longer have him near my daughter. When he returned, I thought to call on the police. He appeared inebriated, however, and I simply thought he'd go home and wear it off."

"Apparently, he didn't," Taryn said.

"Apparently not."

"So, what do you need from me?"

"I don't *know*," he said again.

"What about your wife?" she asked.

His face softened then and he hung his head. "She isn't here. She has never been here. I felt her spirit leave the premises the day she passed."

"I'm...sorry?" Taryn wasn't exactly sure how to respond to that.

"I am sure that, wherever she may be, she's causing an abundance of excitement and merriment," he added sadly. "She certainly did that when she was *here*."

"I would like to help you. I can't think that you're just hanging around here because you don't know how to move on," Taryn said. "You certainly seem like someone who knows what to do."

"I take it you no longer think I went on a murdering spree and killed those around me?" he asked wryly.

Taryn felt herself blush. "You, uh, know about that?"

"I try not to be rude, but I hear a lot. At least where *you* are concerned."

"Then why are you here?"

The air around Julian flickered again and he suddenly looked withdrawn and tired. "If you can determine that, it would be good of you to tell *me*."

And then he was gone again.

FOURTEEN

Holland House, RPH (Hazel Green, Kentucky)

The power continued to be out into the next morning and afternoon. Taryn thought about driving into town but it was Saturday. The electric office was closed. Charaty's mother, who was suffering from breast cancer, had come down with pneumonia. Charaty had called her several days earlier and told her that she was staying in Manchester at the hospital with her. Taryn had asked her to take the week off. Bridget was out of town and her replacement had missed her appointment. Taryn was all alone.

Except for Julian.

She'd been feverish yesterday–feverish and in pain that the morphine had barely touched. She still felt the effects today. Was it possible that she'd imagined the whole thing? After he'd vanished a second time she had called him back and he hadn't returned. She'd fallen asleep and slept through the night. Upon waking the entire thing had felt like a dream.

Taryn's condition had caused neurological issues: brain fog, confusion, memory loss, and even seizures. Was it possible that she'd suffered a stroke?

Taryn sighed.

The lake unfurled before her, an expanse of motionless gray. Taryn sat on the bench and watched it barely lap the sides of the shore. She thought of all the bad things that had happened on and around it. Thought of her aunt nearly drowning in it. Had Julian saved her? She certainly didn't think *he'd* been the culprit holding her under.

Taryn had sworn to herself that she wouldn't return to the water's edge but she'd needed to get out of the house. The air was cold and white today. Even the trees and grass appeared to have lost their color. No wonder she felt so muddled–she lived in a world of literal fog.

When Taryn started to chill, she began walking back up to the house. She'd wrapped an afghan around her shoulders and it was now dampened from the water that hung in the air. Her teeth were chattering when she reached the porch. When she made to turn the knob, however, it wouldn't budge. Taryn pushed on the door but it remained tightly shut. She hadn't brought her key with her; Taryn hardly ever locked the door.

Frustrated now, Taryn walked around the house and tried the other doors. All of them were locked.

Once she was back at the front again, Taryn stood in the front yard and studied the house. What was going on? She couldn't help but feel a measure of anger. She'd loved that house, had dreamed of living in it. Now it was turning against her.

"What do you want?" she cried. "You keeping me out now?"

Miss Dixie bounced against her chest in solidarity.

Taryn flounced back up the porch stairs and pounded on the door. "Julian! Julian, let me in!"

No answer.

Don't you just hate it when your ghost won't listen to you, she thought with irony.

Taryn tried pushing on the door with all her weight. Tried prying open some of the bottom windows. Nothing

161

worked. She was locked out. She couldn't even go anywhere in her car since her keys were locked inside. She considered walking down to Larry's house, but she didn't think her hip and knee could make it. She'd barely been able to walk back up from the lake and now she was hurting again from slamming against the door.

With nothing else to do but wait, Taryn slid down the house and rested her head against the wall. She brought the afghan tighter around her chest and closed her eyes.

What felt like hours later, she awoke from a light sleep to the sound of the key turning in the lock. The door was already creaking open by the time she got to her feet.

As Taryn marched inside, her bones rattling cold, she was *not* amused. "Julian," she called. Her voice rang out soundly through the house. "We need to talk."

*   *   *

"IT WAS FOR YOUR OWN GOOD."

Taryn stoked the fire and then rocked back on her heels. "You keep saying that," she called out over her shoulder. "But I am not sure you know what it means."

"I was helping you," he said.

"By trying to kill me with hypothermia?"

162

She moved back over to the   where she settled against the soft cushions. She was still chilled from her outside adventure. Julian, in the same clothing he'd worn the night before, stood in the doorway with his back to the foyer.

"There are some things you do not understand," he said.

"I keep asking you to explain them to me and you don't," Taryn complained.

Julian sighed, clearly exasperated with her.

Great, Taryn thought, *I even have the ability to piss off ghosts.*

"I don't understand them either," he admitted. "But I can feel them. I understood that it was in your best interest not to come inside so I did something about that."

"So now you're protecting me?" she asked.

Julian looked surprised. "I always protect you," he said.

"*How?*"

"I see you chilled at night," he began, "so I keep the fire going for your warmth. When the other comes, I've created distractions to help you leave the area where you might be harmed. When you were a child and you lost your doll, I found them for you and left them were you would see. When your plug-in lights have failed, I've made them bright again so that you would not be left in the dark."

"Back up again," Taryn said. She would think about those other things later. "What do you mean about the 'other'?"

"I do not see them," Julian said, "but I feel their presence. And their motives are not admirable. They would hurt you."

Taryn bit her lip, worry coursing through her. So there were two things going on in Sarah's house—Julian and something else. And whatever this other thing was, it might want to kill her.

"Do you know about my photos?" she asked. "That I can sometimes see into the past?"

Julian nodded. "Some. I do try not to pry."

A thought occurred to her. "Would you like to see them? The pictures?"

His eyes seemed to light up. "Yes indeed."

Her laptop still had a little charge in it so she powered it up and set it on the coffee table. "You'll, uh, have to come over here," she gestured.

He didn't quite walk like a person, but he didn't exactly fly either. Julian more or less hovered to where she sat cross-legged in the floor. When he bent down beside her, she held her breath. She wasn't sure what she expected from his nearness—to feel overwhelmed perhaps. It felt surprisingly normal, however, to have him so close. In some ways, she guessed he had known her all her life. And, because he had known Sarah, they shared a sort of bond between them.

"See," she began as she turned back to her screen. "This here's the room we're in right now. In this picture, it looks normal."

He nodded.

Then she flipped to one upstairs. "But in this one, you can see that it looks the way it did in, uh, your time I guess."

Julian smiled, his face coming alive with amusement. "So it does! Well, I haven't seen that in many, many years."

Taryn was tickled at his reaction. "There," he pointed to his wardrobe. "That belonged to my mother. I took it with me when I built this house. My wife adored it. Oh, and the washstand! That was a wedding gift."

Taryn pointed to the slip. "And this?"

"Nora's," he replied, his face falling a little. "She'd left it there for after Delilah's birth. Had sworn she would fit back into it. She left it there for, er.."

"Inspiration?" Taryn supplied. "Yeah, in these days we tape magazine pictures to our refrigerators and save super models to our Pinterest boards."

He turned and looked hard at her. "I have no idea what you just said."

Taryn laughed.

Julian had grown quiet, however, and when Taryn looked down she realized that she had moved on to the image of Delilah's room. He brought his face closer to the screen and it took on a bluish tint. She could almost see through it; his face didn't look completely solid.

"You, uh, okay there?" she asked.

His mouth was set in a grim line. "She always had trouble keeping her room tidy," he said in response. "The maid was forever up in arms."

"What happened to your maid?"

Julian sighed and sat back again. It appeared as though he touched the edge of the sofa but a fine, thin line of light separated them.

"There were problems at the end," he said. "With Delilah."

She sits in the chair and stares, Taryn thought to herself.

Julian sharply glanced up at her and glared.

"Did you, uh, hear that?" she asked nervously.

He nodded. "One of those blasted things they said when she was alive."

She had to know, though. "What kinds of problems?"

"They said there was something wrong with her, that she was not 'right.'" His face grew dark and clouded with anger. "They were wrong! She was perfect. *Perfect*."

Taryn didn't press now, but she would have to later. She had a feeling that whatever was up with Delilah then had a strong bearing over what was happening *now*.

She was about to comment on the state of Delilah's room, to assure him that it was clean by any time period's standards, when he sputtered and looked away.

"What's wrong?" she asked anxiously.

"It's that day," Julian whispered.

"What do you mean?"

"The fire." His voice was weakening now and the air was starting to flicker.

"How can you tell."

"The ribbons on the chest of drawers," he answered. "I've given them to her early that morning. A birthday present."

Then he was gone.

Taryn remained on the floor, trying to remember if they'd been there in her dream as well. She was almost certain they were.

*   *   *

THE CELLAR SMELLED RANK AND COLD. It felt as though it hadn't been opened in a very long time, even though Taryn made fairly regular trips down there for supplies.

She didn't want to be there now but she'd ran out of batteries and candles. With the power still off, she wanted to gather more before it grew dark again.

With the last few rays of sunlight streaming through the shadowy room, Taryn scurried across the floor to the metal cabinet that held the extra candles. Sarah had stocked up enough for the zombie apocalypse and now Taryn busied herself filling up the grocery bag she'd brought with her.

Something scuttled in the darkness but she tried to ignore it. With her back to the middle of the room, Taryn quickly filled the bag with candles and then moved to the batteries. Somewhere behind her, she heard a sharp intake of breath.

She'd been feeling safer with the thought of Julian in the house but she knew that what she was hearing wasn't him. He'd said he wasn't trying to scare her and she believed him.

When Taryn turned, the sight that met her had her dropping the paper bag, candles spilling out and rolling around her feet.

A child-size rocking chair moved gently on the small dirt mound in the center of the floor. It creaked rhythmically, the sound growing louder and louder until it was a ringing in

Taryn's ears. The auburn-haired child that sat stonily in the chair looked hard at Taryn, her expression blank. From where she stood, all Taryn could see were the whites of her eyes, milky and stark. The muddy white dress she wore was torn and shredded in places and brushed the ground every time she moved forward. Her hands were curled into claws on the armrests, the fingernails ragged and caked with dirt.

As Taryn watched with mounting horror, her frozen smile was slowly replaced with a slow, grim sneer. It cracked her face open like a porcelain doll.

"She sits in the chair and stares." The disembodied voice floated across the room and was followed by cruel laughter.

Taryn bent down, grabbed the grocery bag, and began to run for the door. She felt like the devil himself was on her heels.

FIFTEEN

Wolfe County, RPH (Kentucky)

The pounding at the front door had Taryn waking up with a started. Disoriented, she reached for her phone to check the time, forgetting that it was dead.

Dead. In her grogginess, Taryn thought of the child in the rocker again and shook.

The knocking came again, but this time it was followed by a voice. "Miss Magill?" came the muffled shout from downstairs.

That was no ghost playing tricks on her, that was a real person.

Taryn quickly jumped to her feet, grabbed her robe, and ran down the stairs. When she got to the door, she was surprised to see the same police officer from the night before standing on her porch.

"Hello again," she said as she invited him inside. "Everything okay?"

"Just doing a welfare check," he explained as he stepped inside. "Everything okay?"

Taryn stood back as he began to walk through her downstairs, looking into corners and around the rooms as though searching for something.

"It's fine," she replied. "What's going on?"

"Your friend Nicola called into the station. Said she hadn't heard from you in several days and that the last time she'd talked to you, you hadn't been well," he said. "Said she tried to call you but you didn't answer."

"Oh," Taryn laughed. "Yeah, sorry about that. The power's been off from the storm and–"

"What storm?" he asked, interrupting her.

"The one from the other night." She took in his look of disbelief before continuing. "It threw the power off and it hasn't come back on yet. My phone died and..."

She watched as he walked over to her lamp, leaned down, and flicked it on. When he straightened and gazed curiously at her, she felt herself growing warm. "Must have just come back on," she said.

"Ma'am, we haven't had any storms lately," he said. "Not for a few weeks."

Taryn had no idea what to say to that. It had stormed almost every night for the past month.

"Are you sure you're okay?"

She nodded numbly.

"Honestly, a woman being up here by yourself, it's not real safe. What if your phone did go out? And with the problems you've been having..." He leaned forward and looked at her with grandfatherly concern. "You sure you don't need anything?"

"I'm fine," she said brightly.

He started for the door. "Well, just make sure you call your friend and let her know everything's okay. And make sure you keep that phone charged!"

Once he was gone, Taryn leaned against the wall in the foyer and sighed. "Julian," she called, "the power wasn't even out."

"That wasn't me," he answered back. She didn't see him, but he sounded like he was standing right next to her.

Taryn opted against telling him about the cellar. She had a strong feeling *that* wasn't him, either.

*　　*　　*

"NOT SLEEPING ANY BETTER?" Lori offered her a refill and Taryn gladly accepted.

"It's been a long few days," she said.

"Well, hopefully it gets better soon," Lori said sympathetically.

Once she'd retreated to the kitchen again, Taryn took out the book she'd been reading and began thumbing through it once more. She'd ordered a whole stack from Amazon a few weeks prior in an attempt to put order to what was going on.

When Taryn had first started seeing the past in her pictures, she'd tried getting on the internet to find others who could do the same. But while she found mediums, psychics, and millions with their own personal ghost stories, she hadn't found a single other person with her ability. For a while she'd thought what she was doing was a fluke, something only limited to the house in which she was working. Indeed, she'd been unable to recapture the magic on the next several projects. But then it had happened again. And again. And again. Still, she'd yet to connect with anyone who could do the same.

Now, as she read through the book about true hauntings, she failed to find a single case in which the person being haunted could actively communicate with the spirit. She'd watched the ghost hunting shows, had seen them get out their little machines and ask their questions. Occasionally, the entity would respond with a fuzzy word or phrase. Sometimes the ghost hunters would go crazy at the response, repeatedly playing it in amazement. Sometimes Taryn didn't hear what they were hearing at all.

This was different. Not once had she seen a person have an active conversation with a physical entity who not only replied but showed reactions through facial expressions and body movements.

Once again, Taryn thought she might be having a stroke. And yet...

Was it crazy that she *liked* Julian? So far they'd only discussed things like dying and the dead, but she got a good feeling about him. She could almost see what he might have been like in life. She found herself wondering what his personality had been, what kinds of things he'd done for hobbies, what his relationship with Delilah had been like.

Basically, she sounded like any other woman who had just experienced a good first date.

And then she thought about his "protection" of her. How he'd watched her through the years. It was funny, but other than Matt, he was the only person still around who'd known her since childhood.

And he wasn't even alive.

Still, she felt a connection with him. The older she got, the more important it was starting to become to her to be around people who remembered her. Did it matter that the person that remembered her was already dead?

"You look like you're in a good mood," Taryn said when Lori returned to her table.

"I am, actually," Lori replied. "My parents got good news. They sold their house today for above the asking price. Now they can retire and they promised to give some of the proceeds to me and my husband to make a down payment on ours."

"Wow, that's great!" Taryn said.

"It really is," Lori agreed. "House has been on the market for two years. Not a single offer and then two on the same day. Crazy, huh?"

Well, Taryn thought as she watched Lori walk away, *at least someone is having a string of luck.*

SIXTEEN

Wolfe County, RPH (Kentucky)

The three officers roamed around her property, talking into their radios and making notes.

Taryn waited on the porch and steamed. She'd been gone only two hours and had returned to find every single first-floor window broken. Although nobody had done anything to damage the inside of the house, and it didn't appear that they'd stolen anything, she was still looking at a few thousand dollars' worth of damage.

"You have insurance?" the oldest of the officers asked.

She nodded. "Yeah. But it's still going to be a pain in the ass."

"Well," the younger one began as he bounded up the stairs and joined them on the porch. "The good news is that we arrested someone about an hour ago, and took him in. There's been a string of robberies in the county and he's admitted to a few of them. Probably be that he's responsible for this one as well."

"Might even be the culprit from the other night," the older one offered.

"Well," Taryn said, "that's good." And it was good that they wouldn't be bothering her anymore, but it still didn't take away the fact that her windows were broken.

"If I were you, I'd stay someplace in town night," the younger officer said. "You don't want to be up here by yourself with these open."

The glass place wouldn't be open until the next morning and the officers were probably right. Taryn was irritated. She'd finally been run out of her home.

Once they'd taken her statement and left, she was left standing in a mess of glass shards.

"At least you weren't here when it happened," she told herself. "It could have been worse."

It could always be worse.

Once they'd taken her statement and left, she was left standing in a mess of glass shards.

"At least you weren't here when it happened," she told herself. "It could have been worse."

It could always be worse.

Once they'd taken her statement and left, she was left standing in a mess of glass shards.

"At least you weren't here when it happened," she told herself. "It could have been worse."

It could always be worse.

*   *   *

JULIAN STOOD IN THE CORNER of the room and watched her pack her suitcase.

"And you didn't see it when it happened?" she asked.

"As I told you, I saw nothing," he replied. "I heard a faint tinkling and then didn't awaken until I heard you shrieking your obscenities outside."

"I'm sure it sounded louder than 'faint tinkling'," she grumbled, throwing a wad of socks into her bag. When she

179

turned to her drawer and began to pull out underwear, she turned and glared at him. "You mind?"

"Pardon me," Julian apologized and closed his eyes while she finished.

"I'm done," she said.

He moved over to where she stood and considered her thoughtfully. "I'm angry too, you know. It's my house as well."

"I know," she sighed. "I'm sorry. It's just, don't you think it's weird that the glass was broken from the inside? Not the outside?"

"Yes," he nodded. "As though someone were trying to get out and not in."

"I guess it was just someone trying to be mean," Taryn said. "I am starting to think it wasn't the person they thought it was. If it was someone breaking in, they would've come and gotten what they wanted and left. Not taken the time to break eight windows."

"I agree," Julian said. "And I would hope that if they return you'll get out that little gun you keep by your bed and make it difficult for them to do it a second time."

Taryn laughed. "You would do that, wouldn't you?"

He nodded. "I don't exactly have a good memory of someone coming in on *me*."

"I guess not."

She was technically ready to go but hated to leave if he was appearing to her. "It would be awfully helpful if you could've seen something."

"I know," Julian said, "but as I told you, I'm not here unless you are. I can't explain it, it's just what is."

"I had no idea I was so powerful," Taryn grinned.

"I had a *little* of an idea," Julian smiled.

"So, what did you do for fun when you were alive?"

"I enjoyed fishing," he replied. "Music. Dancing."

"You danced?" Taryn tried to imagine him moving gracefully across the floor. Actually, it wasn't that difficult to envision since it was basically what he did *now*.

"I had to win my wife in some manner."

"You played the piano, didn't you?"

He nodded. "I was not the player my wife was, but I did enjoy it. My mother insisted I learn."

"That was you I heard playing the other night. A waltz."

His eyes twinkled. "I always enjoyed a good waltz. Besides, I'd been listening to your music enough. It seemed fair enough."

"My music is good!" Taryn protested.

"Some of it," he replied mildly. "Some of it not."

"It's just because you don't understand it. You'd like it if you knew it."

Julian laughed. "I catch on quickly, trust me. And I still dislike a portion of it. But don't work yourself into a tither over it. I am partial to the song about having a worried and jealous heart. The one that sings of loneliness."

"'The Speed of the Sound of Loneliness'," Taryn supplied. "I knew you liked that one. Whenever I played it, you quieted down."

"So my plan worked," Julian chuckled.

Taryn laughed. "I like that one, too."

"Loneliness brought on by choice," Julian mused. "I imagine we've all been there."

Thinking of Matt, Taryn sighed. "You have no idea."

It was starting to grow dark and she knew she needed to get on the road. "I hate to leave now but I really must get into town. Will you, uh, be okay?"

Julian was already starting to fade. "I imagine I'll live. Or not."

She could still hear the echoes of his laughter even after he was gone.

SEVENTEEN

Estill County, RPH (Kentucky)

"*So, the inn I checked into* for the night is supposedly one of the most haunted places in the state of New Hampshire."

Nicki sent peals of laughter through the phone. "Well, have you seen anything yet?"

Taryn took a long look at the gingham curtains, matching bedspread, and profusion of white wicker furniture crammed into the tiny room. She was feeling like she'd been sucked back in time in a totally different way now.

"Not a thing," Taryn laughed. "The only thing haunting me is all these lacy doilies.

"Have you tried Miss Dixie yet?"

Taryn reached over to the small table in front of the window and grabbed her camera. Balancing her phone on her shoulder, she snapped several pictures and then watched the playback. "Nope, nothing," she reported. "Kind of glad, to tell you the truth. The last thing I really want to see is something that happened in a hotel room in the past."

Nicki laughed again. "Well, if it helps, you're sounding better."

"You know, even though my house was broken into and crashed, I *am* actually feeling pretty good." She started to tell Nicki about Julian but hesitated. Taryn felt silly even thinking about it. Things like that didn't happen in real life, not to her or apparently to anyone. She still needed time to think about it. It was still perfectly reasonable to expect that she was suffering from a psychotic break.

Still, Nicki must have read at least part of her mind. "Are you still thinking that the Julian man killed his kid and took a few others down with him?"

"No," Taryn replied, probably a little too quickly.

"New information?"

"You could say that." *Like, he told me himself...*

"So what's your focus now?"

"I'm not sure," Taryn said. "I guess I need to figure out if it's a person harassing me or something else."

"Hmmm..." Nicki hummed in thought for a few seconds and when she spoke again, her voice held excitement. "Hey! The guy that might have burned down your house? You know, a long time ago? He got any descendants?"

"I don't know," Taryn replied. "Why do you ask?"

"I don't know. Could be a revenge thing or something. His great grandfather killed the Aldermans years ago, and now he thinks he must kill you, too. Maybe?"

"I see why you're thinking that but nobody was ever arrested or punished for that fire. Even in the history books they chalk it up to the storm. Julian's pretty much the only person who knows for sure that it wasn't an accident." Taryn refrained from revealing how she knew this tidbit of information and Nicki didn't ask.

"I don't know, Taryn. Don't ever estimate the value of ancestral lines when it comes to this kind of thing. Kinship is powerful. So is destiny. You might be working with something a lot bigger here than you think," Nicki warned her.

Yes, Taryn though, *that's what I am afraid of.*

*　　*　　*

TARYN THANKED THE WOMAN WHO LED HER INSIDE.

"I know you're not normally open right now but I keep missing you," she apologized. "And I really need to look at a few things."

The president of the historical society was in her late fifties. She had shoulder-length, wavy brown hair and a pinched nose. She was probably in her late forties and did not appear pleased by Taryn's presence. Still, she'd allowed her access to the resources for an hour and Taryn was determined to be positive.

"Just because other people are jackasses doesn't mean you should show them up," her grandmother had always told her.

"Can you tell me what, exactly, you're looking for?" Beverly Combs asked in an I-have-better-things-to-do tone.

Thinking that the fire might be the key to understanding what was going on, Taryn had originally wanted to research it. That didn't feel right, now, though.

"I'm actually interested in a few different things," she began. "Any tragedies or murders that have occurred here, for one."

"Since when?" Beverly inquired, folding her arms across her flat chest.

186

"Since ever?" Taryn supplied helpfully.

Beverly stalked off to a back room leaving Taryn sitting alone at a small desk in the front. There was a large map of the surrounding area on the wall and Taryn walked over to it and looked. She found the lake and was able to spot her house on the far side. It was surrounded by greenery for trees. She had to laugh–the map made it very clear that she was out in the middle of nowhere. Larry was the closest neighbor and even he was a thirty-minute walk on a good day.

What *had* made Julian want to move his family so far out of the way?

Beverly reemerged ten minutes later with a stack of books and newspapers in her arm. She spread them out on a conference table in the middle of the room and Taryn joined her. "I've earmarked some passages you might be interested in," she said, gesturing to the books at the end of the table. "Was there something else you wanted?"

"Benjamin Warwick," Taryn said. "Can you tell me anything about him?"

"Had a farm on the lake," Beverly replied. "Farm manager for the Aldermans. When he got laid off he found a job at the mill. Went on to become foreman. He's buried up at Lavonia."

"Did he have any children?"

187

Beverly shook her head. "One child. It died in infancy. Wife passed a few years later and he never remarried."

"Was there any kind of history of violence or crimes or..."

Beverly straightened and brushed a strand of hair behind her ear. "A few scuttles here and there, like any man would have, but nothing serious. He was an upstanding citizen. His farm's part of the summer camp on the lake now."

With that, she turned and disappeared into the other room again, firmly shutting the door behind her.

Taryn sighed with frustration. Was Julian wrong? Maybe Benjamin didn't have anything to do with the fire at all.

An hour later and she had much more information than she'd wanted. As to what she could do with any of it, or what it meant, she didn't know.

EIGHTEEN

Kancamagus Highway, RPH (New Hampshire)

"*Tell me those numbers again,*" Julian demanded of her.

"You're abnormally bossy for a dead guy," Taryn complained.

Julian stopped pacing and sent her a scornful look. "You've known many dead men?"

"A few."

"How many murders?"

Taryn glanced back down at her notes. "Between 1750 and 1861, there were 1,210 killings."

"Solved?"

"Eight hundred," Taryn reported.

"So we have more than four-hundred baffling deaths?"

"Correct."

Julian raked his hands through his hair. "Seems excessive, does it not?"

"For a place of this size, yes," Taryn agreed. "Infant mortality is also extraordinarily high here, as is admittance to mental hospitals."

"I should have left for Boston when I had the chance," Julian grumbled.

"Probably."

"Return to what you referred to as the 'weird things'," Julian ordered.

"Well, you've had six destructive tornados. One wiped out half the town. Two earthquakes. Terrible flooding. Then, of course, there were the fires. Lots and lots of fires and, for what it's worth, most of them were actually caused by lightning. Not, er, like yours."

Julian shook his head as though to clear his mind. "Coincidence?"

190

"I'm not sure I believe in coincidence anymore," Taryn replied. "I worked a project in Wales where something similar had happened. It was the land. We don't know what's causing it, but there is definitely a pattern there."

"Could this be the same then?"

Taryn shrugged. "It doesn't feel the same. In hindsight, I didn't feel the same way there as I do here."

She took another look at the dates again. "There is a period of quietness, you know. From around 1850 until 1895 not much happened at all. I don't know what to make of that."

Julian walked over to her and peered over her shoulder at the timeline she'd made. "There's another one as well," he reported. "From 1950 until around 2013."

"Maybe it takes a fifty-year break every now and then?" Taryn suggested.

Julian suddenly looked troubled, however. "Perhaps..."

When the CD stopped playing, Taryn got up and put on another. Within the first few chords Julian had his hands over his ears. "What in heaven's name is that awful noise?"

Offended, Taryn put her hands on her hips. "It's not 'noise'," she retorted. "It's Bon Jovi."

Julian grimaced. "I have no idea as to what you just said but that's terrible."

"That's my childhood," she retorted. "But since you look like you're going to jump through the roof, I'll change it. You're clearly not ready for anything this exciting."

She fumbled around for something lighter and settled on one she thought they could both live with. "Here, try this."

After a few seconds, Julian removed his hands from his head and simmered down. "This isn't terrible. I don't know what it is, but I rather like it."

"It's Willie Nelson singing with Tom Petty. 'Goodnight Irene,'" Taryn supplied. "I thought this would be more up your alley."

"Up my *what*?"

"Never mind."

With a momentary peace between them, she returned to her seat on the floor by the coffee table. Julian stood by the fireplace, the scorching heat having no effect on him. Soon, he began to sway back and forth in time to the music. "Now this is wonderful," he sighed at last. "I'll see you in my dreams."

Taryn cradled her head in her hands and watched him. "Do you dream?"

"Sometimes," he shrugged.

"What do you see in your dreams?"

"Sometimes you," he answered. "Sometimes I see what you are doing here in the house. And sometimes my wife."

"Do you miss her a lot?"

"It's been many years," he sighed. "It was hardest that first year. Everyone around me urged me to remarry. To 'move on' as they called it. They claimed I needed a mother for Lila. She *had* a mother."

"They did the same to me," Taryn said. "When my fiancé died."

Julian walked over to where she sat and slid down to the floor across from her. "I know about him," he admitted, "a little."

"How?"

"Sarah mentioned your name and the tragedy. I could hear. I am terribly sorry."

Taryn leaned back and closed her eyes. "You know, sometimes I'm not sure if I miss him or if I just miss what could have been. In my mind, in my memory, he's become..."

"Larger than life?" Julian supplied gently.

She nodded. "Yes. It's difficult to say how much of what I miss is Andrew or the idea of him."

"I understand. When Lila was a little girl I often thought of Nora. I imagined how much easier it would have been, how wonderful our life would have been, with her here.

193

And perhaps it would have been and perhaps not. We will never know."

It was nice for Taryn to talk to someone that understood.

"Andrew took care of me. I'd spent most of my life taking care of my grandmother, watching over my best friend Matt. Trying to please people. Trying to remain quiet and good and polite so that people wouldn't want to get rid of me. I didn't have to do that with Andrew. I could be myself and he liked it."

"Well, I like you," Julian smiled. "Sometimes."

She laughed and opened her eyes. "My best friend, Matt, it was different with him. He loved me, I know he did, but I'm not sure he ever really saw *me*. He saw what he needed and what he wanted me to be, but..."

Embarrassed now, she stopped.

"Yet you were going to marry him," Julian prodded her.

"Maybe," Taryn agreed. "But it wasn't right. I was only doing it because he was my friend I cared about him. Because I had spent years feeling like I wasn't really living and I suddenly felt like I wanted my life to start."

"Those are not bad reasons."

"They're not good ones either."

Julian grinned. "So you are a romantic then?"

Taryn shrugged. "I didn't think I was, but maybe I am!"

"It's okay," he said conspiratorially, leaning closer to her. "I am too. Don't tell anyone."

For some reason this sent Taryn into peals of laughter. Who was she going to tell?

"Lila, she saw things," Julian said suddenly.

His face was so serious that Taryn's laughter came to an abrupt stop. "What kinds of things?"

"Things that scared others. Things from the past, not unlike you. And sometimes things from the future." He looked sadly down at his lap and sighed. "They prayed for her, trying to cure her, but it seemed to make it stronger."

"She was psychic?"

"That's probably the proper word for it."

"She'd get her own series today," Taryn said. "It's kind of 'in' to talk to the dead."

"As you would know," he smiled weakly.

"So that's why you sent people away?"

"Yes," Julian nodded. "People were talking about Satan, about demons. They claimed she was unholy. I was afraid for her."

"I'm so sorry."

"She didn't need anyone but me anyway," he said sharply. "I took care of her."

"I know you did." By habit, Taryn reached out to pat his hand. Her fingers felt heat but little else. She brought them back, slightly embarrassed at what she'd done.

"It's fine," Julian sighed. "For a moment, I also forgot who I was and where I am."

"There's something bad here, isn't there?" she asked.

He nodded.

"And I am meant to make it go away?"

He bobbed his head again. "I believe so, yes."

"If I make it go away, will you leave too?"

"I don't know."

Taryn suddenly found herself feeling very lonely again.

*　　*　　*

"I TRIED NOT TO MESS UP THE HOUSE TOO MUCH," Taryn said.

Charaty walked through the downstairs rooms with a keen eye, searching for dust and dirt she'd missed on the first two rounds.

"You did well," she reported. "I've seen worse."

Taryn took that as a compliment.

She'd woken up that morning inspired to paint. It was the first time she'd felt like painting in months. Although her trembling hand made it difficult for her to do the smallest of details, she was still quite proud of what she'd done so far. It was too cold to set up her easel outside so Taryn was working from the pictures she'd taken of Sarah's house. She'd done hundreds of paintings of other people's houses—it was high time she made one of her own.

"How's your mom?"

Charaty, who was now pushing a broom through the foyer, paused. "Strangest thing actually," she said. "They think they have the pneumonia under control but the cancer seems to be in remission. We had no idea. She had bloodwork and a scan coming in two weeks but they went ahead and did them early. The news was not expected."

"Well that's great, right?"

Charaty beamed. "She lives to fight another day."

Taryn put her brush down for a moment and formed the words she'd been trying to find all morning. "Hey, I've been wanting to ask you something."

"Yes?"

"Have you ever felt anything here? Or thought there might be something wrong with the area? With Lewisboro?"

Charaty did not hesitate. "Yes and yes."

Taryn straightened and her heart began thudding in excitement. "Really? What have you felt?"

"There has always been an uneasiness in this house," Charaty replied. "It's why I work so hard to clear the air. Brush all the evil outside, as my mother would say. And the town? Growing up we used to joke about who would make it. Who would live to see thirty."

Taryn was taken aback. She hadn't quite expected Charaty to be so forthcoming.

"But I believe it's improving," Charaty confessed. "The house especially. I come in now and there's a nicer feeling, more brightness. I like to think it's my diligent work."

"It probably is," Taryn agreed.

"Everything goes in cycles. Nothing lasts forever. Even our town is improving. We have the new grocery store going in. Tourism is up. Football team might even make it to regionals this year, who know." Charaty grinned, revealing two crooked front teeth. "We haven't in twenty-five years, but it could happen."

"What do you think causes it? The bad?"

"Well, the Indians certainly had a problem with it."

Taryn felt like groaning. "You mean there's like a Native American burial ground around here?" She didn't think she could deal with a poltergeist.

"No, the opposite," Charaty told her. "They would not put one in here. Claimed there was something wrong with the ground. So they knew."

She began sweeping again and Taryn thought the conversation was over. She returned to her canvas and started painting. A few minutes later, however, Charaty stopped and called out to her.

"Darkness doesn't always have a reason, not like it does in the movies. Sometimes it just *is*."

"And how do we get rid of it?" Taryn asked.

Charaty shrugged, the dust pan bobbing in her hand. "With light."

NINETEEN

North Conway Village, RPH (New Hampshire)

"*I am so sorry,*" Bridget gushed. She removed the blood pressure cuff from Taryn's arm and grimaced. "I should have been here."

"I've been okay," Taryn assured her. "Just that one really bad day."

"Well, your BP looks good anyway. Whatever you're doing, keep it up!"

Taryn smiled secretly to herself. She wondered how her nurse would react if Taryn told her the truth–that her stress levels had been down thanks to her daily visits with her own personal partner in the afterlife.

"So how are you doing?" Taryn asked.

Bridget yawned and stretched her hands over her head. "Tired. Vacations aren't what they used to be."

"I always need one to recover from one," Taryn confessed.

"You and me both, sister," Bridget agreed. "And my darling mother must have called me fifteen times a day to check on me and fill me with random information. I swear, I should have never shown her how to set up a Facebook account. If she's not keeping me up to date on her Candy Crush scores, then she's telling me what Joe Schmo had for dinner."

Taryn laughed. "What does your mom do?"

"She's on disability now," Bridget replied. "She worked at the same place for almost twenty years but she's been retired for a long time now. She needs a damn hobby, is what she needs."

"I started painting again," Taryn said. She pointed to the canvas in the corner of the dining room. It was halfway finished.

"I saw. It's good!" Bridget beamed proudly. "You're very talented."

"Thank you. It's good to have something to do. Now that I'm not working on the house I was getting kind of restless."

"I bet. Stress management is a big part of your therapy. Keep it down and it will help your pain management and your blood pressure," Bridget said.

"I was thinking about going down to Boston for a few days," Taryn said. "You think I'm up for that kind of trip? I didn't know about driving with the medicine pump. I mean, driving that far…"

"I'll have to check with the doctor," Bridget said. "I'll get back to you on that in the morning. If you can't drive, then you might think about the train."

That sounded fun, actually. Taryn loved trains.

By the time Bridget left, Taryn was feeling upbeat. Her blood pressure was level, she'd had a manageable pain day, and she'd even had a bit of an appetite. Things were almost looking up.

*   *   *

"WHY DO YOU KEEP THAT DOOR CLOSED?"

Taryn glanced over her shoulder at the room down the hall and shrugged. "I have no desire."

"Because of before?"

"Yes."

Julian, who had been standing by the window and looking out at the sunset, turned around to face her. "Do you not like your mother?"

Taryn finished folding her laundry and began putting her clothes away. "My mother was okay. She was...distant, I guess you could say. Both of my parents were intellectuals, kind of cerebral. They didn't know what to do with me. My existence barely registered with them."

"How could they possibly not know you were there? Between your impossibly loud music and the way you carry on, chattering to yourself, you're loud enough to wake the dead," Julian grinned.

Taryn stuck her tongue out at him and tossed a sock in his direction. It landed at his feet. "Now what am I supposed to do with that?" he asked with scorn.

Chuckling, Taryn walked over to where he stood and bent over to pick it up. When she straightened, Julian held out his hand to her and placed it by her shoulder. She felt searing heat. It didn't burn her; indeed, it was the kind of warmth she might have experienced from a tanning bad or a roasting day in the sun. There was no physical pressure on her shoulder at all. Julian quickly looked away from her and back to the window.

"Do *you* ever go in that room?"

"The room has no meaning for me," Julian answered. "I sometimes venture near the door but there's a sensation there I am not fond of. It's more difficult for me to manifest around it."

"How come you're able to look almost completely alive now but, before, you were kind of fading in and out?"

The last of the sun disappeared and there was nothing left to see outside so Julian turned back around. "Because of you, I think. The stronger you grew, the stronger I became."

"I don't understand."

"I believe it's because of the pictures you took. Once you could see the past come alive, you started believing in the house. And then in me," he explained.

"Did you have anything to do with the pictures?" Taryn asked.

"No," Julian replied. "I can do very little, to be honest. And not always when I want."

"Seems kind of sad that you've just been waiting around all these years, trying to communicate with someone."

"It's had his drawbacks," he agreed. "But I got plenty of rest before *you* showed up."

"You missed a lot, you know," Taryn grinned. "Movies. Swing dancing. Microwave ovens. *Elvis.*"

"What is an Elvis?"

"What is Elvis?" Taryn scoffed. "You mean you didn't pick up on that over the years?"

"Your aunt didn't chatter to herself as incessantly as you," he pointed out.

"Elvis is the king of rock and roll," Taryn cried.

"Like that terrible music you played the other day?" he asked in scorn. "No thank you."

Taryn's eyes grew wide. "Oh, come on! 'Hound Dog,' 'Love Me Tender,' 'Jailhouse Rock'? Even you would like some of that! And then the movies! You *have* to see 'Viva Las Vegas.' It's a classic."

Julian raised his eyebrows. "You seem awfully excited about these things. I'll take your word for it."

"Uh, no," Taryn said. "You will *not*. We're going to rectify this right now!"

With new motivation, she turned and began marching out the door.

"Where are you going?" he cried from behind her.

"To educate you, you dolt!"

Running down the stairs, she could hear him grumbling behind her. Taryn snickered and soon the house was full of her laughter and his muttering. To an outsider, they would have looked like a couple teasing one another on a night spent inside.

"Hunka Hunka Burnin' Love" was going at full volume when Julian appeared in the living room. He stood back by the fireplace, his arms crossed, and his dark eyes narrowed as he haughtily watched her dance around the room.

"Just *what* are you doing?" he demanded.

"I'm dancing!" Taryn cried over the music.

Singing along with the music, she waved her arms around in the air and twisted her hips as she moved in circles back and forth across the living room.

"That is *not* dancing," he grumbled.

But not even Julian could resist the king and soon his foot was starting to tap the floor and his shoulders were moving back and forth in time with the music. By the time "All Shook Up" came on, while he wasn't exactly dancing, he'd certainly loosened up.

"It's not bad," he finally relented with a grin. "I don't mind this Elvis."

"Ha!" Taryn shouted.

And then, to Taryn's shock, he did begin to dance. Unaccustomed to the rhythm and movements, his body was stiff and awkward at first but what he lacked in style he made up for enthusiasm. Soon, he was flying across the floor with

Taryn, her long hair streaming behind her and the air around him flickering and shimmering.

By the time the song came to an end, they both collapsed on the floor in front of the fire, their laughter echoing around them. They lay head to head, their bodies stretched out in opposite directions. With the heat from the fire and the room spinning above her, Taryn closed her eyes and enjoyed the moment.

"I've watched you do that before," Julian confessed. "I had no idea it was that much fun. We should do that more often."

"We should," Taryn agreed.

And though they weren't touching at all, Taryn felt closer to him than she'd felt to anyone in a long time.

But time. Time was not her friend. She could already feel it closing in around her.

TWENTY

Clark County, RPH (Kentucky)

Taryn was shocked at how clear the lake was. She thought that if she were out in the middle of it, she still might be able to see the bottom. Without a single wisp of fog and the sun high in the sky, it didn't even look like the same body of water. For the first time since reading Sarah's journal entry about her experience in the lake, Taryn didn't feel any kind of ominous dread as she sat on the bench and watched the tiny ripples move towards the bank.

She was almost finished with her painting. She could have finished that afternoon but something had held her back. She wasn't ready, she guessed. If she was working on the rendering of Sarah's house, she had a purpose. After all, she was clearly failing when it came to her other job–the one in which she was meant to figure out what was going on with the house and why Julian was hanging around.

"I don't want to see him go," she whispered aloud. She knew he couldn't hear her. Julian didn't leave the house; he couldn't. He was very respectful of her now and knew when to leave her alone, when she needed privacy. Although he occasionally visited her without her asking first, he always made sure that she didn't want to be alone before he invited himself in.

In an ironic twist of fate, Taryn was finding herself dreading Julian's departure more than she'd dreaded Matt's. Now, on the bench, she thought back to the evening when she'd told him goodbye. It hadn't gone anything like she'd imagined.

Taryn had meant to go down to Florida and talk to him in person. She'd bought a plane ticket and they'd made plans for her to fly down for the weekend. And then he'd had a meeting in Houston and had to abruptly leave that Thursday night. Taryn had canceled her flight. Matt had been totally understanding about it, even offered to pay her back. So, Taryn had planned on flying down the next weekend instead.

And then, the following day, she received what she now thought of as The Package.

When Matt and Taryn had first taken their relationship out of the friend zone and into something more, she'd started going down to Florida on a more regular basis. Sometimes he'd come to her in Nashville and sometimes she'd visit him. She generally flew. Taryn had always found the planes to be chilly so she'd bought a pretty little pink fleece blanket from Kohls. She'd intended to reserve it for flying but it had been so comfortable and so soft that she'd ended up using it for everything. Matt began calling it "Taryn's furry friend" because she had it with her just about everywhere she went in the house. She'd curled up under it on the sofa while they watched television, had used it as an extra blanket on their bed, had rolled it up tightly and used it as a cover-up in the chilly cinemas...She really did love that thing. It became synonymous with her visits.

When things started becoming more serious and her visits to him grew longer, she'd began taking more belongings with her when she went to him. Soon, she had a couple of dresses and pairs of shoes in his closet. She left a few pieces of jewelry behind here and there. Framed a picture of them and put it on his desk. The house was his, for sure, but sometimes she stayed for weeks at a time. It was kind of nice having something of *hers* there.

On her last visit, she'd intentionally left it behind. Left it draped over the edge of the sofa, the white side facing outwards so that it didn't look too girly. "Forgetting something?" he'd asked.

"Nope!" she'd replied cheerfully.

In the week before The Package arrived, Matt had called her. "Hey," he'd said, "you left that book here that you were reading. Did you mean to?"

And, to be sure, she hadn't.

"Crap," she'd replied. "I forgot it. I guess I'll just download it or something."

"I'll mail it to you." That was her Matt. He was always organized and efficient.

"Thanks!" She'd been pleased that he would take the time to send it to her.

"Oh, and your blanket is here, too. I'll send it as well."

Taryn had been taken aback. She'd thought her intentions were obvious. "No, I meant to leave it," she explained. "It means I'm coming back!"

Matt hadn't understood. "But don't you want it? I thought you loved it!"

"I do love it. That's why I left it. It being there means I'm returning. It's kind of like leaving your shoes in front of the fireplace or something."

Matt had been quiet at that. She wasn't sure he'd understood.

"Well then," he'd finally said, "I'll just fold it up and put it in the closet."

Taryn had been upset at that. She'd felt as though Matt didn't want a part of her setting out in the house. She knew he was a neat freak, that Matt liked everything in its place, but it was just a simple blanket. And it was a part of *her*.

A few days later, the book had arrived in the mail. Along with her blanket. Taryn took it as a sign. She'd called him almost right away.

"I'm sorry Matt, but I need to talk to you..."

In the end, he'd come across unruffled by her words. He'd assured her that he loved her, that he would always be there for her, but he hadn't tried to talk her out of it. They might as well have been talking about the weather.

Taryn had hung up the phone feeling both heartbroken and completely underwhelmed. It was a strange combination.

She missed their conversations. She missed the feeling of security with him. She missed the familiarity. She missed the way he was always there for her.

But she wasn't sure she missed *him*.

Taryn sighed and rose to her feet. The sparkling water had soothed her, despite her reminiscing. She was feeling good when she began climbing the hill up to her house.

When she got to the top, however, she stopped in her tracks.

Her car had been totally trashed. All four tires were slashed, the sides were keyed, and the windshield was smashed completely in. It was folded in half, like a sheet of paper. She'd never seen anything like it.

"Well I'll be damned," Taryn cursed, rage building inside her. "Shit! Dammit to hell!"

For the next several minutes she let every curse word she knew ring over the mountainside. As Taryn yelled, she bounced around the vehicle, seething with each section of damage she saw. Red blood swam behind her eyes. She could feel her head growing hot and wet from the livid sweat that ran through her hair and down her face.

"Damn you!"

When the rapping came from her bedroom window, she looked up and saw Julian staring down at her. Taryn hopped from one foot to the other as she gestured wildly at her car. "Look!" she shouted. "LOOK!"

Julian miserably nodded his head in commiseration.

When she'd screamed out everything she could, Taryn let out a defeated groan and started walking towards the house.

Another call to the police, she thought wryly. *The insurance company is going to love me.*

* * *

The grandfatherly officer patiently regarded Taryn with kind eyes.

"Ma'am," he began gently, "are you sure you want to be up here by yourself?"

She couldn't, of course, confess to him that she wasn't truly alone.

"I'm fine," she replied. "But I guess if the other guy is in jail then it means he's not the one responsible for this."

"Is there anyone out there who might be angry with you?" he asked. "Anyone who might stand something to gain by hurting you?"

"I hardly know anyone here," Taryn replied. "I've only been here for about six months and I barely get out of the house."

He nodded. Then something else flickered over his face and for a moment Taryn wondered if he believed her at all.

"You, uh, have some medical issues, I understand?"

"A connective tissue disorder," Taryn replied. "It puts me in a lot of pain and makes my internal organs prone to rupture."

He bobbed his head again, his gray hair bouncing up and down. "And does that, uh, cause any problems with..." His face reddened as his words trailed off.

"Yes," she answered through clenched teeth. "It does cause some neurological issues but not the kind where I would destroy my own property and not remember."

She wasn't sure he looked convinced.

"Well," he said as he got to his feet. "The good news is that it looks like they left a book of matches behind. With any luck, there will be some prints on it that we can use."

Taryn wasn't feeling optimistic when they left.

"First the windows, now my car. What's next?"

"For just a second I thought I saw someone," Julian said. "I wish it could have been clearer."

"Don't worry about it," Taryn sighed. "At least you believe me. You know I didn't do this myself, right?"

Julian nodded sympathetically.

Taryn dropped down to the sofa and groaned with frustration. "I just don't know what to do, Julian. I know I'm meant to be doing something but I can't figure it out. What is my purpose here?"

Julian, for his part, looked pained on her behalf. "I am sorry that everything is so trying for you right now," he said stiffly. "I feel like it's my own fault."

Taryn gestured to the spot on the sofa next to her. "It's not your fault. I should be doing more for you."

Julian lowered himself to the cushions and she felt the slightest of movements. "You gave me some life again. Without you, I wouldn't be here. It's enough."

Without you, I'm not sure I'd be here either, Taryn thought to herself.

Together, they sat in silence. They continued to be lost in their own thoughts until the sun sank and they were left in the lavender of twilight.

TWENTY-ONE

Kancamagus Highway, RPH (New Hampshire)

"*I knew you were an artist but I guess* I wasn't expecting you to be..."

"Good?" Taryn supplied.

Charaty shrugged. "Ever since those digital cameras got cheaper every Tom, Dick, and Harry has been calling themselves photographers and charging an arm and a leg for weddings."

"I take my pictures for fun," Taryn said. "My art has always been in my paintings."

"Well," Charaty pointed at the canvas, "the old place never looked better than it does on your canvas. Looks like it's brand new. And like you could walk right through the front door."

Taryn felt a surge of pride.

"Looks like you're almost finished," she said.

Taryn nodded. "Just about."

"Might get you to do one of my house when you're done. Not as grand as this one, of course, but it's a nice little farm house that goes back away."

Taryn said sure, why not? She'd need something to do once she was finished.

While Charaty scurried around the house with her cleaning rituals, Taryn rested on the sofa. She was tired. Her dreams had been unusually vivid the night before. She hadn't rested much. She'd awoken once to find Julian sitting in the chair in the corner of her room, watching her with concern. He hadn't spoken to her. When she'd finally given it up that morning and gotten out of bed, she'd called to him but he hadn't answered. She hadn't seen him since.

"You got plans for the weekend?" Taryn asked when Charaty came back through the foyer.

"Fishing with the husband," Charaty answered.

"Oh yeah? Where do you all go?"

"About half a mile around the lake from your dock down there," Charaty motioned in the general direction of the lake.

"I didn't think there was good fishing in that lake..."

Charaty shrugged. "Didn't used to be. People been getting lucky in the past few weeks. Thought we'd try our hand at it, too."

"Well, good luck," Taryn told her.

"I catch something, I'll bring you some."

Taryn wrinkled her nose. "I, uh, appreciate the effort but I have no idea how to skin a fish or de-bone it or whatever it is you do before you eat it."

Charaty shook her head in mock sadness. "Whatever are they teaching you young women these days? You think all fish comes in a square from the golden arches?"

Taryn's housekeeper was not that much older than she.

"How's your mom?"

"Out of the hospital now," Charaty replied. "At home, ordering everyone around."

Taryn had leaned back on the cushions again with her eyes closed and was listening to Charaty vacuum the area rug in the foyer when she was suddenly struck with a thought.

"Charaty!" she called over the road of the machine.

When she appeared in the doorway, she didn't look happy. Charaty did not like to be interrupted when she was in the middle of something. "Yes?"

"Did you know my aunt?"

"I knew of her," she replied. "I didn't have her in school but some of my friends did. Now my mother, she knew Sarah. She used to work up here as a housekeeper for a few years."

"Oh yeah? What happened?"

Charaty shrugged. "Gracefully let go. The 'gracefully' part is my own addition, not what my mother called it."

"Ouch." Awkward.

"The official reason was that Sarah could no longer afford to keep paying her."

"The unofficial?"

Charaty pursed her lips and considered her answer thoughtfully. "I realize she's your family but there were many people that considered her to be a *difficult* woman. Difficult to know, difficult to get along with."

Taryn nodded. Her own mother had certainly said the same about her sister.

"It was hard on our family for a while. Mother's work was out only source of income. I was a teenager and ended up getting a job over in Lewisboro. Nothing here to speak of in this township, of course. Got my GED. But we managed," Charaty smiled thinly at the last part.

Taryn didn't ask any further questions after that.

*　　*　　*

SHE STOOD AT THE VESTIBULE AND LOOKED. The porch was gone. When she turned and looked down through the yard, she noticed that only some of the walkway was complete. There were no trees, no mountains. It was a white abyss beyond the greenery of the lawn. Taryn trembled with apprehension. Something was wrong.

The door was open, beckoning her inside. She quietly slipped through the opening, moving silently. She knew she wasn't meant to be there.

Everything looked different inside. Her area rug in the foyer was gone. It had been replaced by a colorful runner. A library table with fresh flowers was up against the wall; a large oval mirror hung over it. Taryn could not see her reflection.

A snatch of yellow fabric fluttered by her. It was a blur of color. Taryn saw shades of auburn flying behind it.

Giggling.

Taryn walked down the foyer towards the master staircase. Heavy work boots waited at the bottom. She crouched down and ran her fingers over them. Mud caked off in her hand. She straightened and clenched her fist, letting the clump of dirt crumble between her fingers, heard it raining down on the floor.

Taryn began climbing the stairs. Up and up she went until she reached the top. The smaller hallway was there, undisturbed. Taryn ignored it for now and chose the master bedroom instead.

Inside, the slip still lay on the chaise. The ribbons, folded gently on the bureau. Waiting for Delilah.

The feeling of dread sliding over here, chilling her skin. Something watching her every move, weighing its options. Taryn could feel it all around her but could see nothing.

Delilah's room.

Why had she not been in her bedroom that night, Taryn wondered. *If she'd been in her own room, would they have lived?*

Again, she walked to the window and looked out. Delilah running and laughing. Julian running after her, teasing her.

And then, again, he paused and looked up at the window. Their eyes met. He saw her. There was no recognition. Instead, she saw fear. She raised her hand to wave but he'd already turned his back to her and was running away from the house.

*   *   *

"YOU WERE DREAMING."

Taryn nodded and dipped her brush in the paint again. "I was dreaming about you."

Julian came over to where she sat and studied her canvas over her shoulder. "Was it a good one?" he asked mischievously.

"Sure it was," she answered with a smile. "I scared the tarnation out of you."

"I don't frighten," he said haughtily.

"Could've fooled me. You looked like you'd seen a ghost."

Taryn was working on the background. She'd yet to add the complementary scenery to her painting. As it was, she'd almost finished the house itself but at present time it was floating in the air.

"Julian, why was Delilah in the servant's room that night? Why not in her own room?"

Julian grunted. "You wouldn't believe me if I told you."

Taryn looked over her shoulder at him. "Yeah," she scoffed. "Because nothing weird has ever happened to me."

He rolled his eyes at her.

"It was my wife," he said at last. "I felt like she gave me a sign."

"What kind of sign?"

"It doesn't matter," he shrugged. "I just didn't feel comfortable leaving her in her bedroom so I moved her for the night."

Taryn wasn't sure if she should say what she was about to. But she forged ahead anyway. "If she'd been in her own room that night..."

"Yes, we probably would've gotten out," he agreed. He raked his hands through his hair, his curls springing up all over his head with his action. "It's my fault."

"Only one person set that fire," Taryn pointed out. "And it wasn't you."

"Believing in ghosts got us killed."

"Believing in ghosts brought me to life."

They considered one another for a moment, their eyes not leaving the other's face, and then she looked away.

"You said I was dreaming," she said once she'd returned to her painting. "Was I tossing and turning?"

"I don't know," Julian replied. "I couldn't see you. I saw you only when you awoke. You looked troubled, the way you do after a bad dream."

"What do you mean you couldn't see me?"

"I don't know," he replied. "I was aware of being here but I wasn't awake. It's the same as when you leave the house."

Taryn would have to think about that. When she was dreaming soundly, did it mean she wasn't there? Or that at least that her consciousness wasn't really there?

"You said you got a sign from your wife that night. Did you ever see or feel her after she died? Before, you, before *you* died?"

"No," he replied sadly. "Never."

"Never got a sign that she was still hanging around, checking in you guys? Never felt her spirit? Nothing?"

"Nothing," he echoed. "Once she was gone, she was gone."

"It seems unfair," Taryn sighed. She dipped her brush into the green on her pallet and began working on the trees in the distance.

"Yes," he agreed, "it does. How about you? Do you ever see Andrew?"

"Never," Taryn said. "Not once. It's awfully unfair that I can see other random dead people but not someone I love. No offense."

But Julian *did* look a little wounded.

"What about Sarah?" she asked, changing the subject. "Did you ever see or feel her?"

"Once," he said. "But it was about you. For an instant, I felt her return. She was concerned about you. I felt her concern, felt her in the house. I woke up for a brief moment. Then she was gone."

And yet it gladdened Taryn to know that the link between her and her aunt was still alive. She'd felt her once as well, while working a job in Kentucky.

"Do you look forward to leaving?" she asked.

"No."

Taryn looked up from her brush in surprise. "'NO'? You want to keep hanging around here with me?"

Julian smiled gaily, his face lighting up. "Does that surprise you?"

"Well, yeah."

He laughed. "I've grown a little fond of you over the years. It happens."

"Why?"

"Your idle chatter about everything. How lost you get in your paintings and your pictures. Your incessant music playing. You dance when you cook."

"I do not," Taryn retorted.

"You do so," Julian argued. "I've seen it. You dance when you clean, too. You talk to yourself and seem to listen. I've never quite seen anyone do that before. You care about everyone and I do mean everyone. You worry about your friend Nicki. You worry about your friend Liza. You worry about Sarah and Stella and Matt. Oh, how you worry about Matt! You'd go back to him in an instant, not for your *own* sake but because you worry about him being alone."

Taryn frowned. "Well, as lovely and exciting as you make me sound, I would think that the gates of paradise would be more alluring."

Julian shook his head. "I have no idea what awaits me there but I am perfectly content with knowing what I have *here*."

Taryn blushed.

"What about you? Do you not feel the need to go into town? To see one of your idle movies? To go away for the night and see an exciting show or walk through one of your many museums?" he challenged.

Taryn shrugged and arrogantly lifted her head. "I'm *busy*."

"You like me. You like my company," he said with a laugh.

"Maybe."

They waited a beat and then both broke out into peals of laughter. Neither felt nor saw the blackness that had begun to close in around the house.

TWENTY-TWO

Portsmouth, RPH (New Hampshire)

"*I actually thought I was doing* better," Taryn sighed.

Dr. Fannin laid the chart on the stool next to him and frowned. "In some ways, you're very stable," he agreed. "Your blood pressure is stable, for instance. It's down from the last time you were here and your nurse says it's been steadily decreasing. Naturally we don't want it too low, of course, but it's fine as it is. Your pain level seems to be more manageable with the pump."

"It's better than the pills," Taryn said.

"Your potassium is dangerously low. I have something I want you to drink in a few minutes. It's not pleasant, but it will help. I am also concerned about your magnesium and Vitamin D levels."

"Is that all?" she asked hopefully.

"Your CT scan shows an increase in the aneurysm," he finished. "Even from six months ago. And we're noticing the abnormalities on the echo. Those things are not good."

"Are they fixable?" Taryn smiled weakly.

"Sometimes," he replied. "Surgery is sometimes an option once it reaches a certain size. In your case, however..."

"It would probably make things worse," she finished for him.

"I don't know that your body could handle the stress of it," he said gently.

"So, what are doing then?" Taryn asked. "Just waiting around until I die?"

"Taryn, it could be years before anything happens," Dr. Fannin reminded her.

"Or it could be tomorrow," she said darkly.

He did not disagree with her.

"I'm going to give you something to help control the heart rate," he said. He quickly began scribbling something on a prescription pad. "How is the medicine I prescribed for anxiety working for you?"

"It mostly knocks me out," she said. "I don't like it."

"Well, take it sparingly. Sleep is one of the best things for you right now."

"I don't want to sleep away whatever I have left of my life," she grumbled.

Dr. Fannin smiled. "I don't blame you."

"What about traveling?"

A shadow passed briefly over his face. "You want to keep the stress levels down. Traffic, carrying luggage, dealing with crowds...it all depends on how you handle such hassles. If you think you can easily move past some of those struggles that get the best of us, then by all means–travel away!"

Taryn smiled. Ironically, even now that she knew she could, she didn't want to leave the house.

*   *   *

IT WAS A NICE AFTERNOON and Portsmouth was looking particularly pleasant in the sunshine. Taryn stopped at a waterside café and enjoyed two lobster rolls as she sat outside and watched the boats in the harbor. It was a lovely meal and she finished it off with a scoop of ice cream.

By the time she made it to her car, however, she was sick to her stomach. Taryn emptied its contents by her front right wheel. The sound and smell just made her vomit harder.

The drive home was difficult. Along with her queasy stomach, her hips were aching from all the walking around she'd done on the cobblestones. Before lunch she'd wandered into a used book store and secondhand shop. She'd bought herself a mystery and a pair of vintage cowboy boots to replace some she'd lost in the tornado/fire. Now she was paying for it.

The road back to Sarah's house felt incessantly long. The road was unpaved and thick with mud. Each time Taryn turned off onto the driveway, she felt she was entering another dimension. The towering trees closed in around her, soaring above her and her little car. Each time she inched along the narrow road, she prayed she wouldn't get stuck. The woods that enfolded her were dense and soundless; in the springtime when she rolled down her windows she couldn't even hear the songs of the birds.

When she pulled up to the house she was sweating from exhaustion and pain. Her hips were throbbing and her legs ached from the pressure on her muscles. She had to stop and vomit again at the edge of her porch and some of it got in her hair.

Taryn entered the house cross and drained.

"You're home earlier than I thought you'd be," Julian remarked from the living room.

She'd noticed him watching her from the window; she knew he'd seen her throw up. Taryn was embarrassed. She didn't even like watching herself throw up. At night, she kept the lights off in the bathroom so that she wouldn't have to look at her stomach contents in the toilet.

"I got sick," she barked. "Sorry I wasn't gone longer."

"That's fine," he answered mildly. "What did the doctor say?"

"Nothing *good*," she snapped again.

Julian looked slightly stung but he raised his head high and ignored her attitude. "I gathered that."

"I just want to be myself, okay?" Taryn kicked off her shoes, tossed her purchases on the floor, and began dragging herself up the stairs. She went into the bathroom with the intentions of running herself a nice, hot bath but she wound up kneeling by the toilet again.

The pain was growing increasingly worse. She could barely stand. On shaky legs, pale and exhausted Taryn stumbled into her bedroom and collapsed on the bed. The room began spinning wildly and Taryn gripped her pillow for support. In the corner, she could see her canvas. It was almost finished now, she just had to finish the mountains, but the sight of it made her cry. Remembering the day before, a day in which she'd felt fairly good, and thinking of how she'd sat and laughed with Julian had her sobbing. The worst part of being sick was knowing you had no control over it. Sometimes remembering the good days hurt harder than going through the bad ones. She was a prisoner in her own body.

"No, you don't," Julian said from beside her.

She didn't have to roll over to know that he was on the bed next to her.

"Now I don't *what*?" she whispered feebly.

"No, you don't want to be alone," he said.

She couldn't feel him but there was a slight pressure on the bed, as though something were gently pressing down on the other side. He moved closer to her until the light that emanated from him, always felt but never seen, began warming her back. Neither spoke but after a while the tears stopped falling and, in the warmth and comfort of having someone close, she fell asleep.

TWENTY-THREE

Glyndon Hotel, RPH (Richmond, Kentucky)

Julian was gone when Taryn awoke. She found herself feeling so guilty that she couldn't even call for him. After taking a shower, she stumbled around the house, trying to paint or take pictures or even read, but she couldn't concentrate. Finally, she gave it up and went into town.

Her pub didn't open until noon. The Chinese restaurant she sometimes ate at was under renovations for the upcoming winter. There weren't a lot of other options. Her own tiny township didn't have anything in the way of restaurants and North Conway was too far to drive. Lewisboro would have to do it. After driving around for ten minutes, she finally came upon a waterside inn that claimed to have a restaurant open for breakfast.

The Coke tasted funny and she was almost certain that the stuffed crepes were frozen and microwaved but the décor was nice. She read on the back of the menu that the inn had been there, in one shape or form, since 1803. It was also haunted. Of course.

"We're a little quiet this morning," her server (also the hostess) apologized. "You get me all to yourself!"

"I like quiet," Taryn said.

"You live here?"

Taryn nodded. "I do now."

"Yeah, I figured. Most of the tourists are already gone for the season."

The middle-aged woman hadn't said a whole lot but she was friendly. Taryn was never one for complaining about food she didn't have to cook and dishes she didn't to clean. While she'd had better meals in Lewisboro, she was glad she'd come out.

"How bad do the winters get up here?"

The woman, who'd been sweeping up on the other side of the dining room, stopped. "Sometimes bad," she answered. "We can get ten inches dumped on us at once. The good news is that they're usually good about clearing off the roads fast enough. You shouldn't have any trouble."

Taryn snorted. "Not where I live. I don't think they even clear my road at all."

"Oh yeah? Where's that honey?"

"The Alderman stone house up on the mountain?"

Her server let out a slow whistle. "I'd say you're in trouble. You got you lots of firewood?"

"I think so," Taryn nodded. "I'm just planning on not getting out this winter. I'll see you in the spring thaw."

The other woman laughed. The sound was eerie in the otherwise empty dining room. "Probably not a bad idea."

When she came back to get her check and inquired about the meal, she read something on Taryn's face and laughed. "You didn't like it, did you?"

"Oh, it was good," Taryn said. "I just think the Coke was a little flat."

"It wasn't flat," the woman replied. "It wasn't Coke."

"I'm sorry?"

She scurried away and came back with a two liter of generic cola. "Those big tanks you put in the Coke machine? They're too expensive. I'm saving up for one but, in the meantime, I just use these."

Well, Taryn thought, *you learn something new every day.*

She could see the lake from where she sat in the window and her mind was on paying and going out for a walk when the server came back for her change. She had tuned everything around her out and was barely listening until the word "Alderman" caught her attention.

"I'm sorry," Taryn apologized. "I was daydreaming. What did you say?"

"I asked if you knew anything about the history of the house you're living in," the other woman replied, unruffled by Taryn's lack of attention.

Taryn laughed to herself. *Did she ever.*

"This inn here was originally owned by the Bennington family," her server said. "Prominent family here in town. They helped settle the area."

Taryn nodded patiently. She'd read the name in her searching.

"Nora Bennington married the man that built your house."

Taryn straightened, now at attention.

"I know of Nora," Taryn said. "I'm currently sleeping her bedroom. Do you know anything about her?"

The woman shook her head. "Nothing important. They all seemed to keep to themselves after a while. I reckon they had themselves some pretty big parties up there in the beginning but then she got pregnant and..."

"And died," Taryn finished for her.

"Yes, sad things used to happen around here."

"I hear they're getting better," Taryn offered.

"They sure are! You know, we weren't even at capacity over the summer but, starting this weekend, I have the next two weeks booked solid? And fall foliage is over. I don't know what *these* people want!" But she laughed when she said it, her face filled with glee.

Taryn thanked her again and started collecting her knapsack and camera to go. She was halfway to the door when the woman called after her again.

"Oh, dearie! I don't know about anything Nora Bennington Alderman, but I cans how you her picture."

Taryn stopped in her tracks, her heart plummeting to her feet. *What?*

"Excuse me?"

"Her picture. It's in the back on the wall. Come here and I'll show you..."

It seemed to take Taryn forever to walk across the dining room floor. She might as well have been walking through rubber cement. When she reached the other side, she was met with a wall of old photographs. Some were fairly recent and showed the new owners renovating the old inn, standing proudly in front of the sign with their family members. Some were much, much older. Ancient pictures that were yellowing around the edges. Brittle cardboard pictures containing stiff-looking characters with blurry features.

It did not take long for Taryn to find the one she wanted. Nora and what might have been her sisters stood on the front porch of the inn, the lake spreading out like a sheet of glass behind them. The women were smiling. Nora wasn't much more than a teenager. Her hair had fallen from the pins and was blowing loosely across her shoulders. Her patterned dress gently hung to her sides.

Taryn leaned forward to get a closer look. She jolted and jumped back a little. When she turned and looked at her server, she saw that the other woman's face pale.

"Funny, I didn't notice that until just now," she said in a shaky voice. "Wonder how I missed it?"

"Wonder how *you* missed it?" Taryn whispered. "Wonder how *I* missed it?"

She turned and leaned in closer to the image of Julian's wife again.

She could have been looking in a mirror.

*   *   *

TARYN DIDN'T JUST WALK INTO HER HOUSE–she stormed in like a hurricane.

"Julian!" she bellowed at the top of her lungs. "Julian, you come here right *now*."

He was before her in an instant. His dark eyes flashed anger and his mouth was twisted in a snarl. "I'll not have you speak to me in that manner," he barked. "Act like a lady or I *will* leave."

"Oh yeah," Taryn grumbled. "I'd like to see you try..."

She kicked off her shoes and shrugged her jacket to the floor. "And I'm no lady," she added.

"Then act like a human being," he said.

She spun on her heel and faced him. His clothing never changed. It couldn't, she knew that now. He was stuck in the clothes he died in. It had made her very self-conscious about what she wore now. She'd even started taking more care with her night clothes.

Julian was not a traditionally handsome man. He wasn't one most women would take a second look at on the street. His ears and nose were a little too big for his face, his arms and legs skinny and awkward. His thick head of curly hair threatened to overtake his head. He could have been a double for James Frain in "Where the Heart Is," which made her take to calling him "Forney" on occasion.

"What is this *Forney*?" he'd demand. "From one of your ridiculous movies I presume..."

Then she'd made him watch it. By the end, he was tearing up. Had made her rewind the part where Novalee had approached him at the college half a dozen times.

He didn't look like Forney now. He looked like he might like to tear her head off. She felt likewise towards him.

"Why didn't you tell me?" she hissed.

"Tell you *what*?"

Taryn marched through the foyer towards the kitchen. She passed the parlor and dining room with him on her heels. She could feel him stirring behind her. She went to her refrigerator, pulled out a real Coke, and then returned to the living room. He didn't make a sound but followed her every move. Once she was settled on the sofa, Miss Dixie in her lap, he spoke again.

"I don't subscribe to the silent treatment," Julian remarked lightly. "So, you're either going to tell me what's got you in a tither or I'm leaving."

Suddenly Taryn felt like she might break into tears. She could feel her nose stinging, what she used to refer to as "the nose stage" when she was a kid, and knew that the water would begin spilling momentarily.

"You lied to me," she sniffed weakly.

"I did no such thing," he retorted. "I have no reason to lie to you."

"You didn't tell me about your wife, about Nora."

Julian held out his arms and frowned. "I've told you everything you've asked, everything I know. What could you possibly mean?"

Taryn flipped Miss Dixie on and searched for the picture she'd taken of the photo inside the dining room. Once she had it in front of her, she zoomed in on it.

"Come here," she said wearily. "I'm not going to be able to hand this to you."

Julian went to her and knelt at her side. "Look," she commanded.

He leaned in closely, just as she had done at the inn, and then gasped.

"I don't understand," he said.

When he turned and she saw the shock and disbelief on his face, she believed him, too.

"How could you not know?" Taryn demanded.

"I don't know." His voice was high-pitched, as though frightened, and he was paler than usual. Taryn's anger began dissipating as she came to realized that what they were looking at was a shock to him as well.

"Did her looks change or something? Did she used to look different?" Taryn asked.

243

Julian shook his head and closed his eyes. "I can't remember," he insisted softly. "I haven't been able to see her face for years. I remember impressions of her, the shape of her body and the feel of her hair, but I can't see any of her features. Not for a very long time."

"Why?" Taryn whispered.

"I thought it had something to do with my death," he explained. "And then you came here as a child and your face over the years was the only one I could see. Even Sarah's was blurry. I can't explain it."

Taryn leaned back against the sofa and tried to wrap her head around what she was hearing.

"I find the whole thing a little odd," she said at last. "Like, I was a little kid and you were basically a grown man and you were watching me. I mean, isn't that weird? We put people in jail for that these days."

Julian smiled ruefully. "It wasn't like that. You were a different person each time you returned. I wanted to protect the child Taryn. You reminded me of my daughter. Then the years passed and you returned as an adult. You were a different person. Your energy was the same, I knew you were *you*, but..."

"I've changed but you haven't," Taryn pointed out. "If I was your wife *then–*"

"Then you just keep returning to me in different forms," he finished for her.

"I don't belong to anyone," Taryn protested stubbornly.

"No, you don't," he agreed. "But I think I'm *yours*."

"You think that's why you haven't gone anywhere?" Taryn asked softly. "That you were waiting for me?"

"Yes. And I think I've been waiting for a very long time. An eternity really."

TWENTY-FOUR

Botherum House, RH (Lexington, Kentucky)

Taryn was back at the vestibule. The porch was gone.

Colorful ceramic pots sprouting lively flowers flanked the front door. Behind her, the mountains loomed gray and green in the distance. The surrounding woods were thick and dark. She could feel a warm breeze against her bare feet; it drifted up from her toes and billowed her nightgown. When she glanced down, Taryn saw that she wore the same night one she'd worn to bed. Her hair lay tangled down her back, almost brushing her waist. She was groggy from the Ambien she'd taken before bed and was surprised to feel her tummy rumbling from lack of supper.

It was the realest dream Taryn had ever had.

Again, she gently budged the door open and began moving through the house. The wood was smooth and cool beneath her and when she ran her fingers over the wall, she felt the slick paper under her fingertips. At the sound of giggling behind her, Taryn turned and saw Delilah race across the foyer, the hem of her yellow dress flying. She ran out the front door and Taryn felt the vibrations when the door was slammed shut.

Alone in the house now, Taryn began climbing the master staircase. Despite being hungry, her legs and hips were not bothering her. She paused and flexed her feet now, astonished by the lack of pain. Not long ago she'd retired to bed early in part thanks to the agony in her bones and tissue; now she barely felt but a twinge. She smiled at the relief that coursed through her. It was the best she'd felt in ages.

When Taryn reached the landing on the second floor, she waited, trying to decide which way to go next. She was at an impasse here and the need for further exploration was great. She was feeling rather strong, not like she'd wake up at any second, but she didn't want to push her luck.

The part of the house that had burned in the fire was to her left. It won out. Taryn traveled down the short corridor now and soon came to a stop in the doorway of the servant's room where Delilah had died—would die soon. The plain bed was covered in a patchwork quilt. The bureau and wardrobe were simple walnut. Two red bordello style lamps flanked the bed on nightstands. Someone had added a pitcher of daisies on the bureau.

It was the first time Taryn had seen the room. She chilled now, just knowing what would soon happen in it. If she hung around, if she warned Julian of what was to happen that night, would he listen? *Could* she stay that long? Would it even change anything at all?

In her panic, she felt her head begin to spin, her stomach to jump. Taryn could already start to feel herself awaken, begin to feel herself fading away.

She quickly turned and went back down the small corridor and on to Delilah's bedroom. Taryn glanced around, looking for some way to warn them not to move her that night. Paper? A note on the mirror? She couldn't just leave without *trying*.

Before she could find anything to write with, she heard the laughter outside. Again, Taryn went to the window and looked outside. Julian was there, chasing Delilah and making her giggle. Once again, he paused and looked up and saw Taryn. By habit now, she raised her hand and waved to him. The terror shadowed his face, as though he'd seen a ghost, and then he was running away, disappearing around the house.

Taryn stepped back from the window. She could feel herself flickering, was getting tunnel vision and dizzy from her time spent in the dream. She didn't have much time.

Looking frantically around the room for something, *anything*, to write with, Taryn finally saw a sliver of charred wood in the fireplace. It would have to do.

With it in her hand she moved to the wall above Delilah's bed and started to write on the pale-patterned wallpaper.

"Wait." The powerful order came from the doorway.

Taryn turned and saw Julian standing there, watching her with alarm. He looked tanner now, had more color to his face. He wore a coat and dark shoes. His hair, however, was still a curly mess. He still looked like *her* Julian.

"What are you doing?" he whispered hoarsely.

She wanted to answer, wanted to speak to him. She had so much to say, so much she had to do now that they were together in a world where both were in physical form. *Go away tonight. Leave this house. Don't let Delilah sleep in the guest room.*

I love you.

Nevertheless, when she moved her lips she found she was unable to speak. It was as though all the words had

249

disappeared. The sliver of wood slipped from her hand and landed on the bed.

With the room spinning around now, Taryn staggered to where he stood, her arms held out for balance. Flabbergasted, he backed up a foot and held his hands out to her, beckoning her to keep away. In the last few seconds she knew she had, Taryn hurled herself at him and wrapped her arms around his waist. She could feel his heart beating through his chest, feel his warmth through his clothing. His solidness, his *realness*, brought tears to her eyes. And for just an instant he brought his hands to her hair and pulled her closer.

Then she woke up.

*   *   *

"I'M CONCERNED FOR YOU BEING here by yourself," Bridget pronounced.

"That's what the police keep saying," Taryn said.

"Do they have any idea who's been bothering you?"

Taryn, tired from her exercises, plopped down on the dining room chair. "Nope."

"Well I've lived here all my life and I don't think I've ever seen anyone as harassed as you," Bridget said.

Taryn wasn't sure if she was meant to feel shocked or proud.

As Bridget started packing up her tools, Taryn took the time to get to know her a little better. "You ever thought about leaving? I have been to a lot of small towns over the years and it seems that's always the big thing–people wanting to get out."

"I did when I was younger," Bridget told her. "My mother is kind of codependent though. She always pulled the guilt trip on me."

"Ah."

"I was thinking of going back to college though, maybe in the fall," she shrugged. "My little brother graduates from high school then. At least he'll be out of the house and I won't have to worry about *him*."

"Your brother going to college?"

"Yep," she nodded. "He got a football scholarship down in Mass. Hey, did you know they made it to the regionals this year? First time in something like twenty years."

"I heard they were doing well," Taryn said.

"Shocked the hell out of us." She shook her head as though she was still trying to wrap her mind around it. Taryn smiled politely. She didn't know much about high school football but she knew that the other people in town were awfully worked up about it.

Bridget was packed and ready but when she stood to leave she noticed the painting in the corner. "Hey! You finished with it already?"

"Almost," Taryn said. "Some detail work to do."

"So, have you found that the painting has helped with anything? Lessening the stress perhaps? Sleeping better?"

Taryn started to answer, had a whole response that included things about having a hobby and keeping oneself busy, but then stopped when a sudden realization hit her.

The painting…

"It's helped a little," she finally responded weakly. Her heart was bubbling with excitement.

Bridget flashed her a bright smile and waved as she sailed out the door. "See you next week! Whatever you're doing, keep it up!"

If she knew what I was doing, Taryn thought to herself, *she'd have me committed.*

Taryn watched Bridget leave from the window. When she was certain she was in her car and driving away, she called out to Julian.

"I figured something out!" she cried impatiently as she waited for him to emerge. "The painting–"

"Is causing your dreams," he finished for her.

252

Taryn felt a twinge of disappointment. "How did *you* know?" she demanded.

"It came to me at the same time it did to you."

Taryn pursed her lips. The more time they spent together, the more it seemed they were able to do that with one another. The day before she'd finished his sentences twice, much to his amusement.

"The closer I come to finishing it, the more vivid the dreams are," she explained. "That *has* to be it, right?"

"It certainly seems logical to me."

Now she found herself growing excited again. "I couldn't see the mountains and the woods until I painted them," she said. "And parts of the house didn't have details until I put them there."

Julian nodded. "That makes sense. Has it happened to you before?"

"No," Taryn said. "Although I have noticed that when I work with Miss Dixie and things turn up in my pictures, it's a lot easier for me to connect with a place's energy."

"Hmmm..."

"If I paint more," Taryn said now, feeling herself blush, "do you think I could spend more time with you in the past?"

"I wouldn't know you," he said softly, but he looked pained as he spoke. Taryn felt he was keeping something from her, something important. "But we could change that. I'd like for you to try."

"The more I paint, the better it gets."

Julian frowned. "But what happens when you're done?"

Taryn's face dropped as she slid back down to the dining room chair. "I have no idea."

TWENTY-FIVE

Beacon Hill, Boston, RPH

Taryn still wasn't sure what she was meant to do with the information she'd learned about Nora. A few days later, she was still thinking about it. Was *she* Nora? She'd never given reincarnation a lot of thought, but figured it was just as likely as anything any other religion believed in when it concerned the afterlife. Still, she might be playing around with fire with her dreams. Had something changed from Taryn's travels back to the past? Could dreams *do* that?

She'd tried talking it over with Julian the day before, but hadn't gotten the answers she'd hoped for.

"Julian?"

He looked up from the images he'd been studying on Taryn's computer. "Yes?"

"Are you here when I'm asleep?"

"Most of the time," he replied. "You are very restless. I worry."

She got an image of him standing the corner of her room or by her bed, just watching her sleep. While she found the idea almost sickeningly romantic, another side of her hoped she wasn't doing anything embarrassing while she was passed out.

"And when you're not here?"

"I sleep as well, as I have explained."

"Hmmmm." She waited while she gathered her thoughts and then spoke again. "Are there any times when I am here but you can't be?"

He nodded.

"What changes?"

"I don't know," he shrugged. "Two nights ago, when you were dreaming about being inside the house, I couldn't find you. I was here but you were not. Your painting was gone, your clothes were gone. I assumed *I* was dreaming as well. It was all very disorienting. I didn't like it."

The thought was so unsettling that Taryn hadn't worked on her painting since. She had been taking a lot of pictures but, so far, nothing had come of them.

Now, she and Julian sat in her parlor with a small fire glowing from the hearth. Both went back over her pictures from that day, talking about the work that still needed to be done on the house. Julian was full of ideas. In another life, he might have been an architect.

"What did Delilah do that scared everyone?" Taryn asked gently.

Julian looked pained as he turned from the images and looked at her. "She was *right*. That's what she did–she was right."

His words were hard, but his face was soft. She constantly found herself wanting to touch him.

"As in she predicted things?"

He nodded. "There was a fire at the sawmill. She knew a week before. My foreman's mother had a stroke. She saw it before it happened. It's like anything else I imagine; people don't understand what they can't explain."

"Or they get scared if the information doesn't benefit them in some way," Taryn added. "It's all well and good until it stops helping *them*."

Julian nodded his agreement, his eyes flashing dark.

"The witch hunt of our neighbors to the south was long over, but that didn't mean I expected the town to act in a rational sense," he declared. "I should have left with her."

His hand formed into a fist but when he slammed it into his palm, it barely made a sound. Taryn felt a gust of wind, however, that blew straight through her.

I wonder how many other times I've felt such a thing and had no idea it was an angry ghost, Taryn thought to herself.

"It's too late to worry about that now," she told Julian tenderly. She, herself, knew all about regret and how those feelings could eat you alive. "But what if we can go back and I warn you? What if you could get out of the fire sooner?"

Julian knitted his brows. "Do you think you could?"

"I tried last time," Taryn admitted, "but I woke up too soon. Maybe that won't happen this time. I've done more work on the painting since. If I finished it..."

"Not that I wouldn't like to outlive the fire, and to especially see my daughter do so, but what would that do to *you*?"

"What do you mean?" Taryn asked.

Julian patted the floor next to him. Taryn had been going through her aunt's notebooks but now she put those aside and joined him. "Would that not change things?"

"Well, I could hope so. That would be the idea," Taryn said with a grin. "But I don't think it would affect *me*. You'd eventually die anyway, no offense, and my grandparents would buy the farm."

She laughed as she realized the implication of her words. "Well, not in *that* sense."

Julian grinned. Some sayings had apparently withstood the test of time.

"They'd buy it and then they'd leave it to Sarah and I would be here."

"If I lived and remarried? Had a son and left the house to him? Simple decisions could change the course of this history, or our history. Perhaps it wouldn't be possible for your grandparents to buy the farm after all," he countered.

She hadn't thought of that. Still...

"I wouldn't care," Taryn retorted, swishing her ponytail from side to side. "At least you would have lived. You and Delilah."

She thought of the young girl again, of her yellow dress and auburn hair as she ran through the foyer. Heard her laughter as she skipped across the lawn. For one brief moment Taryn felt a pang in her heart. Taryn, who had never had much of a maternal sense, suddenly wished she could see Delilah herself. To know what it was like to love someone that much. To read stories together and eat meals together and cuddle in front of the fire with a little hand in hers…

"It matters that much?" Julian asked, interrupting her thoughts. He looked pleased.

Taryn smiled weakly. "I'll admit, the remarrying part doesn't thrill me but–"

"You're jealous!" he interrupted her, his eyes bright and wide.

"No!" She squirmed nervously and hid her face from him. "Just a little."

"And now you're blushing," he teased her.

"Oh, stop it!"

Julian laughed. "Well, to change the subject. What do you think of *my* paintings?"

"Yours?" Taryn looked up from her arm, her face still pink and warm. "I didn't know you painted."

"Your picture there," he pointed to the laptop.

She leaned forward and looked at the image in which he was indicating. It was a photo she'd taken at the foot of the stairs. The painting of the lake. "*You* did that?" she asked. "It's good!"

"And the one in the bedroom," he beamed.

She flipped to the master bedroom, to the painting of the horses and the mountains on the wall. "I had no idea that you were an artist, Julian."

"Well, I dabbled here and there. It was a pastime."

"Who did the one of Delilah downstairs?"

"That was me as well," he replied modestly. "She wouldn't sit still for anyone other than her father."

Taryn sat back and grinned. "You played the piano and painted. You were quite the renaissance man."

"I *was* quite the catch, wasn't I?" he teased her again. "I shouldn't have any trouble finding another wife if you help me live."

She glared at him and he made to slap her on the knee. When his hand did not make contact, their expressions faded. Taryn felt a wave of disappointment. She couldn't help but remember the men in her past, the ones she'd freely embraced and made physical contact with. At that moment, she'd have given up all of them just to be able to touch Julian.

"Sometimes it's hard to remember why you're here," she said.

"I agree." And then, as though reading her thoughts, he said, "I wonder about those you've touched in passing. The store clerks, the mail carrier, the servers in the restaurant. Those whose arms and hands you've grazed or touched, sometimes without even realizing it. And I am intensely jealous of all of them."

261

She looked up at him and for several seconds they held each other's eyes. Then she looked away. Sometimes it hurt just to look at him. Had she felt that before?

Taryn sat quietly for a moment and then remembered something. "Hey! If I don't have a piano, then how were you able to play that night?"

"I imagined a time in which I could play. It was a simple memory," he explained. "I wasn't actually playing an imaginary piano."

"Can you do that with people? Like, can you remember your daughter's laughter and let me hear it?"

"No," he replied sadly. "I cannot. Like your camera there, it comes and goes. I wish I had the control."

"Sometimes it seems as though you *are* able to touch things though," she said. "Like my toys or blanket when I was a kid."

"I wasn't touching them. I was imagining them relocated. I did not pick them up."

Taryn exhaled noisily; she was searching for any loophole she could find.

Finally, she jumped to her feet. "We're not getting anywhere with these pictures and notebooks. Nothing bad has happened in, like, a week. How about you play me some of your music, I'll play you some of mine, we'll build a fire, and I'll make something good to eat?"

"Something I am unable to have? That sounds dandy," he retorted with a make-believe frown.

Taryn stuck her tongue out at him. "You'll be fine. You can smell it and watch me dance around the kitchen."

He appeared to mull the idea over and then shrugged. "It's a deal," he agreed.

Accordingly, while she played Buddy Holly and skirted around the kitchen to "Peggy Sue" while the spaghetti cooked, Julian rested on a barstool and entertained her with stories about his childhood—back when her part of the world had still been a bit of the "wild west."

They laughed and talked as Taryn tried to imagine Julian a small child toddling around under his parents' feet, getting into sacks of flour and chasing chickens in their yard. He told her of the horses he'd bred, of the long-distance rides he and Nora had taken through the mountains. Of the bonfires they'd built in their yard before Delilah and the parties that had gone on for hours. He described the gaiety of the music, the guests' clothing, and the miles of food they'd set out on exquisitely decorated tables.

"Nora paid attention to every detail," he told her. "Much in the same way you do through your paintings and photos. She never missed a thing."

He told her of their honeymoon to New York and the long train ride they'd endured. Taryn could almost smell the sights and sounds of the city as it neared the dawn of the twentieth century. He talked of waking up each morning and watching the sunrise over the tall buildings. The war between the states had only recently ended and there was an air of excitement and hope everywhere they went. (Being from the south, she'd heard a completely different side before. It was fascinating to hear details from someone who had been there.)

Taryn had him describe the women's clothing, the shops, the carriages and wagons they'd ridden in.

"You wouldn't have liked the shoes," he assured her. "They're nothing like those sneakers of yours that you're constantly kicking off."

"I'd deal," she replied, almost salivating over the idea of Victorian button boots and kid leather slippers.

He shared anecdotes about building the house, of the various designs he'd considered. Hiring the architect to come up from Boston. Nora's decorating ideas and how he'd pretended to be outraged by the cost of all she chose, only to go behind her back and order two of everything she loved. Taryn could feel his excitement as the walls went up and the floors were laid down.

"I was here every day to watch the progress," he said. "Nora would walk through the rooms even before the walls were built. She always brought paper to make ideas of what was going where and how everything would look."

"Was she an artist too?" Taryn asked.

"Of a sense. She had an eye for these things. She saw everything as it could be, not as it was," he remembered fondly. "Like the way *you* can see the potential in the old houses."

Matt had often spoke of his ex-girlfriend, Clarissa. His memories of her exquisite beauty, vast intellect, and winning personality had always made her feel inferior. Julian's stories of his wife did not do the same. Instead, as she listened to his tales, she saw it all and very much wanted to be there for it. Indeed, there were moments when she almost felt like she *had* been there.

While she ate her spaghetti, Taryn regaled Julian with accounts of *her* childhood. Of the adventures she'd had with Matt on their invisible horses.

"We lived in a subdivision with a lot of other houses that looked exactly alike. We had to make up our own adventures," she explained. "Our bikes were our horses. Or sometimes we'd just gallop around without them. And, you know, because I was so short he'd have to help me on mine."

"He just wanted to put his arms around you," Julian countered.

"Oh, come on. He was *nine!*"

"Doesn't matter. Men are men, regardless of age."

Taryn spoke of the awards she'd won in school, of how she'd always gone on the stage to receive them and surveyed the audience to find her parents–and how they were never there. He glowered at this. Then she told him about spending the night in her grandmother's farm house, snuggling against her soft arms that smelled of baby powder and waking up to her movements in the kitchen below.

"It was always home," she said. "And here with Sarah, too."

He had softened at that. "Those times I remember some of."

"I missed Sarah once I stopped coming," Taryn said sadly. "I never understood what happened. I thought she stopped loving me."

"Your aunt still loved you. I believe she kept you away to protect you," Julian said.

"Do you think whatever was here is gone?" Taryn asked. "It's been quiet for a while."

"Evil lurks," Julian said quietly. "It waits. I do not feel comfortable yet."

When she was finished, he had her turn off her radio and he played his music, as promised.

"I can't be here for this," he explained. "But I will return."

266

Taryn retired to the living room where she reclined on the sofa, closed her eyes, and waited.

The music was so soft when it began that she had to strain her ears to hear it. Soon, however, the gentle waltz filled the room as the piano music grew louder and louder. Taryn smiled to herself as the old-fashioned tune spun around her. She imagined herself in a beautiful ball gown dancing through the rooms, her dress brushing the floor with each turn. Her hair tumbling from its pins on her head. Laughing while everyone else swirled around her in a blur of color.

When he was finished, Julian returned. "Does it stack up to your music today?"

"I know that one," Taryn smiled. She sat up and made room for him on the sofa."

"You know Charles Harris?" he asked in surprise.

"I know Irene Dunne," Taryn laughed. "She sang 'After the Ball' in one of her movies."

"Well, I suppose some good things do live on after all," Julian mused thoughtfully. "We must watch that film of yours soon. I *do* have another one for you, however. One my mother used to play."

This time the tune was a melancholy one. Taryn didn't know what the words were, or if it had any lyrics at all, but the longing in the Scottish-flavored melody was clear. The simple ballad floated around her like a breeze, elegant and dainty at once, but Taryn found herself tearing up. When he returned, she was busy embarrassing herself with tears.

"You're right," she said, "I don't know that one. What was it?"

"'Love Next Time' it's called," he replied. "An old song brought over by my grandmother from Scotland. I always found it rather melancholy myself."

"Does it have lyrics? Words?"

"Well," Julian chuckled, "I am not much of a singer myself, but I can try."

He cleared his throat, brushed his hair from his face, and closed his eyes. "Please do not hold this against me. This is *not* one of my talents."

Taryn listened.

"I feel your touch in the sunlight

I know your voice on the air

And though you never speak to me

I suppose that's your affair

Oh distant maid

Beyond the veil

Place your hands in mine

Dance to me through the misty years

And be my love in time.

Be my love this time

I smell perfume in the gloaming

I mourn you cannot care

And though you never wait for me

I suppose that's your affair

Oh unborn love beyond the years

Blend your life with mine

Come to me through the years

And be my love in time.

I close my eyes in the evening

I never held you near

And as I sleep you come to me

And whisper in my ear

Oh ancient love behind my days

I'll blend my life with thine

Reborn with you in another world

I'll be your love next time."

Julian opened his eyes. "I suppose it's a bit of a depressing tune at that, isn't it? The Scots are happy enough to sing about sadness."

Taryn, who felt as though her heart had just bottomed out, couldn't speak. When she finally opened her mouth to say something, a loud *bang* came from upstairs. It was followed by the smell of kerosene and smoke.

"The house!" Taryn cried, jumping to her feet. Before Julian could react, she was sprinting up the stairs, taking them two at a time.

*　　*　　*

TARYN LAY ON THE FLOOR IN THE BEDROOM, beaten and bruised from an unseen assailant. Something had attacked her at the top of the stairs but she hadn't see who. Or what.

Now, as she attempted to get to her knees, something shoved her back down. Taryn coughed and called out for Julian. He didn't respond.

The searing hot pain on her back from where her accoster held her down burned. She struggled against the pain and weight, fighting whatever had her trapped. Whatever detained her was abnormally strong. Gritting her teeth, she kicked and fought, exhausting herself until it felt like all her muscles were screaming in agony.

When Taryn was finally able to flip herself over, the heaviness suddenly lifted from her body and she could breathe. Her breaths came short and raspy–she was still having trouble. The heaviness hadn't yet left her chest. The scent of kerosene and smoke were still in the air, but she saw no flames; there was no fire. There was also no intruder.

"Who's there?" Taryn called out weakly.

Nothing answered.

Her cell phone was on her nightstand and now she wobbled towards it, moving painfully but quickly with the intent to dial Larry and 911. Before she could reach it, however, the wind was being knocked out of her again.

Taryn clutched her curtains as she fell to the ground and the one closest to her landed-on top of her. She screamed as she thrashed against the fabric now being held over her face. The lacy material was shoved into her mouth and she choked on it, gagging when it cut off her breath. Invisible hands slapped and pinched her all over her body as she kicked and hit out with her arms to throw off whoever fought her.

All the while, she continued to call out for Julian.

When Taryn felt herself losing consciousness, his last song flitted through her head. As she began to weaken and her struggling lessened in strength, she closed her eyes and smiled. The lyrics coursed through her, the idea of love through time, and instead of fighting, now she began to smile.

The pressure on her eased. And then it was gone completely.

Taryn opened her eyes and looked around. The curtain was now simply lying atop her and she was able to easily brush it away. When she rose unsteadily to her feet, she was holding the shredded material in her hands but the room was empty. She was all alone.

"Julian!" she blubbered, the tears now freely flowing down her face. Her entire body ached and she trembled in fear, could still feel her body being held down.

When he appeared in the doorway, he looked as though he'd just ran through three circles of hell. His hair was disheveled, his face red with anger. He moved quickly to her, his hands outstretched as though to embrace her. He stopped short when they were close. Neither could touch the other. Now, in frustration, he ran his hands through his hair and cursed.

"I couldn't come," he avowed. "I tried but I couldn't. I heard it all. I could see it in my mind, but I couldn't come!"

"What was it?" she whimpered as she fell to the floor, all strength zapping out of her. Taryn was crying, both from the terror and from the pain quickly overtaking her body. "Who was it?"

"I couldn't *see!*" he shouted again in anger. There was nothing like a man that felt useless.

Taryn rested her back against the wall. She continued to clutch the curtain.

"What are we going to do?" she whispered.

He slid down next to her, got as close as he could. The only thing that separated them was a faint shadow.

"I don't know."

TWENTY-SIX

Glyndon Hotel, RPH (Richmond, Kentucky)

"*I'm going out for awhile,*" Taryn called through the house.

She slung her laptop bag over one shoulder and Miss Dixie over the other.

"Have a good time," Julian called back.

In one way, Taryn felt guilty for leaving him. Julian had nothing to do when she wasn't there and that left her feeling ripe with personality responsibility towards him. He wanted to feel useful, wanted to be *doing* something, but he couldn't without her there.

Taryn, for her part, hadn't had a big desire to leave the house lately. She'd been content hanging around there with him. In fact, she hadn't been out for an entire week. It would be Thanksgiving in a few days. She couldn't believe how quickly the time was flying. They'd already seen some snow. She needed to go into town and stock up on food and supplies before the weather turned bad. And she was tired of cooking.

It was complicated being friends with a ghost.

She appreciated, though, the way he didn't question here when she left. Didn't ask her if she was "okay" to leave or imply that she shouldn't be on the road. He seemed to understand that she could take care of herself, even if he also understood that sometimes she needed companionship.

All the leaves were gone from the trees now. Taryn sped down the two-lane road through the township and headed towards the highway that would take her to North Conway. Her plans were to grab a bite for lunch there and then drive a portion of the Kancamagus Highway. It was meant to be beautiful and if she didn't do it now, the weather and her health might not allow it later. On this small road she concentrated hard to keep from hitting potholes and barking dogs or from going the wrong way around bends that seemed to come from nowhere.

Once on the main road, she began passing unexpected covered bridges, mom 'n pop grocery stores, and gas stations that didn't have "pay here" options at the pumps. These were all mixed in with new Texaco stations, eye-catching Chinese restaurants with dazzling paintings of the Great Wall on the side of the buildings, and modern homes with RVs in the driveway that cost more than her college education. As she'd thought more than once, this part of rural New Hampshire was a land of contradictions.

With Kelly Willis' "Little Honey" rocking on her stereo, Taryn barreled down the road, her heat turned up nice and toasty and her fingers drumming a rhythm on her steering wheel. She was feeling good today and was glad to take advantage of it. She'd booked reservations at the historic inn for Thanksgiving and she had mentioned to Julian about cutting down a live tree for Christmas.

She still wasn't sure what she'd do about him when Nicki and Shawn arrived.

"I don't want you hiding," she'd told him. "But I'm not sure what to say."

"I could just visit you at night, if that would be easier."

She'd grinned at the idea. "Well, that certainly sounds exciting!"

They'd both laughed then and gone back to the movie she'd popped in for them.

Nicki and Shawn might not understand at first, but once they saw Julian and got a feel for the situation she knew they'd be okay. She just didn't want to try and explain things to them beforehand—they'd definitely try to have her committed.

Taryn settled on the little Italian place she liked in North Conway. The fettuccini alfredo and slice of strawberry cheesecake were way too rich for her on a temperamental tummy but she didn't care; Taryn was in the mood to treat herself. While she waited for her food, she pulled out the last of Sarah's notebooks and began to flip through it.

In all, Taryn had gone through more than three dozen notebooks and journals. She'd found very little useful information in any of them but the tidbits she had discovered had given her a clearer picture of the aunt she'd loved. Sarah had been an organized soul, even though, in later years, she was starting to go a little Grey Gardens. She'd kept exhaustive lists of just about everything, from correspondence with family members to her grocery shopping. She'd also kept detailed budgets and information for her taxes mixed in with things from work.

At one point, of a fellow teacher, she'd written: "Cloud has disappointed me to the extent that I am having difficulty sleeping at night. Once a fine teacher, they're now acting completely out of bounds with their students. When the physical assault was reported last week, it was the last straw. I had already filed the report on the unusual and unsuitable forms of reprimands that had been used in the past. Locking students in the coat closets and asking them to reveal embarrassing, and personal, information before their classmates is inappropriate. To think that is just the tip of the iceberg. Well."

Taryn didn't know who "Cloud" was since Sarah had given her co-workers and fellow teachers nicknames in her notebooks. Another one she referred to as "Sticky" had stolen funds from a PTA cookie drive. "Windstorm" had inappropriate relationships with his female students. "Bandit" had a penchant for inviting the male students to her house for "study sessions" that had turned into parties.

Apparently, Sarah had put up with a lot as a principal.

Taryn's fettuccini had just arrived and she was about to put the notebook away when something caught her eye. It was a reference to "Rosie"–the nickname that Sarah had used to indicate Taryn's mother. There had been few references to Sarah's family at all, outside of Taryn, in her writings so she immediately felt compelled to continue reading.

Half an hour later, she was still sitting in shock, her pasta cold.

"You want me to wrap that up for you?" her server inquired pleasantly.

Taryn nodded numbly.

She might never eat again.

*　　*　　*

THE KANCAMAGUS HIGHWAY was known as one of the most scenic byways in New England. It stretched through the White Mountains from Conway to Lincoln. Each year, it saw nearly one million visitors. Taryn was the only one on it now.

The beech, maple, and birch trees had all lost their leaves by now. She'd heard that the thirty-five miles of the road were often sluggish in the fall, from people coming to see the foliage and moose sightings. Now, however, Taryn could skirt along at her own pace. She stopped at several locations to get out and obediently take a picture before returning to her car and traveling on to the next scenic stop. She did these things numbly, dutifully.

The mountains and valleys spread out before her, now brown seas of living organisms. Still pristine without interruption by gas stations, motor inns, or subdivisions, she was left to her own thoughts.

Rain had fallen that morning, real rain and not what she'd been experiencing at her house, and when Taryn stopped at one overlook she could smell the scent of fresh pines wafting towards her. She closed her eyes and held her breath, taking it all in. There was a bench at that spot and she settled onto it now, despite the chill in the air. Another car rumbled behind her, the first she'd seen since leaving Conway Village. It slowed down as though to stop but then sped away at the last minute.

Guess they want to be alone, too, she thought to herself.

Sarah had not been Taryn's aunt. All those years of feeling close to her, of looking up to her and wishing she could live in New Hampshire with her, of secretly wishing that she could *belong* to her and she had not even been Sarah's niece.

She'd been her daughter.

"I regret my decision almost daily," Sarah had written in the last notebook. "Rosie has little kindness and self-awareness within her. My beautiful baby deserves something better. I wish it could have been me."

At first, Taryn had thought that Sarah was simply expressing frustration over her mother's parenting style. It did leave much to be desired, after all. But then there had been *this* entry.

"My mistake was not in having a child, I wouldn't regret Taryn for the world, but in not being strong enough to handle the responsibilities that came with her. I thought I was a different person. I hope she never discovers the truth."

I hope she never discovers the truth, Taryn thought now with disgust. Well, guess what *Mom*?

So, Sarah hadn't wanted her. Rosie hadn't *really* wanted her and had taken her out of, what, loyalty? Duty? It certainly wasn't love. There was no love lost between Sarah and her sister. No wonder her parents had been relieved when Taryn had gone to stay with Stella. They'd probably never wanted a child to start with.

And what was with Sarah anyway? Was it *really* better for her to stay up there in the old house by herself, letting it collapse around her? Dealing with cheating and lying students? Was *that* the life she preferred?

Taryn could feel the anger boiling inside her. They could've had a good life. Even when her parents died, it hadn't been too late. Sarah could've taken her then. She was older by then and would've been a big help.

The feeling of being unwanted, of being alone in the world, that had driven Taryn for most of her life. And it didn't even have to be that way! She'd had a mother, a *real* mother, and that woman hadn't wanted her.

She paused now in her anger as she considered something else. What about her father? Who the hell was *he*?

With a heavy heart, Taryn finally gave it up and returned to her car. The Kancamagus Highway was stunning; she was just too heartbroken to truly see it.

TWENTY-SEVEN

Esmeralda, RPH (Boston Harbor)

It was dark by the time Taryn was on the two-lane road that would return her to her driveway. She couldn't believe she'd been out as long as she had, but then, with the winter closing in on her, the days were getting shorter.

Her drive home wasn't anywhere near as carefree as the drive out had been. The fog grew thicker with each passing mile and soon Taryn had to slow down her car so that she could see the road. There was a wall of white ahead of her and Taryn strained her eyes through the murky light to find the twists and turns of the road. She turned her radio down to a soft whisper for concentration.

She liked to have missed the turn to her road. She could usually see Larry's modular home on the corner but, even with his porch lights on, it was barely more than a blur in the fog. Taryn's car squeaked by the ditch as she made the sharp turn and her wheels squealed in the darkness.

It took her fifteen minutes to travel the driveway. The radio was offering little comfort so she turned it off and began to sing. "Goodnight Irene" reminded her of one of her first nights with Julian so she raised her voice and counted down the number of turns until she got home. He'd be there, then, and she wouldn't be alone. Just a little while longer…

Suddenly, Taryn's wheels jerked to the right and her car began to pick up speed. She was rounding a curve with a steep gully off to her right. Taryn slammed on the brakes and tried to straighten the car, but her steering wheel was locked; it wouldn't budge. She stomped on the brakes again but although her feet hit the floorboard, the car picked up speed.

Taryn screamed and tried again to turn the wheel. Seconds later, she felt the car going down over the embankment. With the tree limbs smacking her newly-replaced windshield and the car bouncing over the roots and rocks it sped over, Taryn was tossed from side to side. In her headlights, she saw the beech tree coming right at her and she braced for impact.

The "thud" had her bouncing in her seat. Taryn's head snapped back and her stomach lurched. But the car had come to a stop.

After gingerly checking all her bones to ensure nothing was broken, Taryn quickly pried open her door and let herself out. The woods were dark, save for the bright glare of headlights coming from her car. She grabbed Miss Dixie and her laptop from the backseat and began to make her way through the brambles and trees to the driveway. Behind her, the headlights still lingered like a sad beacon.

My insurance company is going to hate me, she thought wryly.

Taryn looked when she reached the top of the hill. She looked for something in the road that she might have hit, something that would make her lose control of the car. Of course, she saw nothing.

Sighing, Taryn took a firm grip on Miss Dixie and began the long hike up the rest of the drive, the damp fog chilling her to the skin.

"I DON'T BELIEVE IT," Julian said again, stubbornly.

"I showed you the excerpt," Taryn grumbled. "You know it's true."

He paced back and forth in front of the fireplace, his long legs making him cover the floor in just a few steps each time. "I know what I read but there has to be more to it," he complained. "Sarah would not have just had you and tossed you out like that. There has to be a reason."

"Maybe," Taryn said, "the reason was that she was a single woman with a career and didn't want to be tied down with a child."

Julian paused, considered, and then shook his head. "I don't think so."

"What makes you so sure?"

"I knew her a little and I know you a lot. There's no way in this world someone would get rid of you unless they had to."

"She wasn't the only one," Taryn muttered.

"Look," he came to a rest in front of her. "I had a daughter. Nothing in this world would have made me give her up. Nothing."

"Nothing?" Taryn asked.

"Okay, one thing. Her safety. That's it."

286

Taryn raised her arms. "What did I need saving from?"

"My darling," Julian laughed, "has it not occurred to you that this house and town are trying to *kill* you?"

"And yet everyone else seems to be doing so much *better*," Taryn complained.

"That's true," Julian admitted. "It's true.... So. What are we missing?"

"I don't know," Taryn said. "What are we missing?"

Julian turned back to the fire and faced it. He folded his hands behind his back and Taryn watched his fingers fiddling with one another, a nervous habit she'd noticed in him. She found herself wanting to reach out and touch him, to see what his skin felt like. Was it smooth? Rough? Cold? She wished she'd ran her fingers through his hair when she had the chance in Delilah's bedroom. It looked so silky reflected in the firelight. The inability to just *feel* him was driving her insane.

"Julian, tell me again those dates that where things were kind of slow around here." She had just thought of something.

"From around 1860 to 1890 for the first set," he replied. And then again in–"

The knocking on the door was from a human, not from a ghost.

"The police," Taryn said. "I had to call in a report."

Julian was gone by the time she reached the foyer.

This time, the grandfatherly officer wore a grim expression. "Miss Magill?" he asked. "We think we might know what's going on around your property. Had some officers go down and look at your car. Didn't find much wrong but as we were driving up here, we apprehended a suspect sneaking around your barn in the back."

Taryn stepped onto the porch. "Is everything okay?"

"We're pretty sure they've been stalking you for awhile," he said. "Probably the one responsible for all the things that have been going on."

He gestured towards the patrol car and Taryn flinched in surprise. There, handcuffed and being directed into the back seat, was Larry. When he met her eyes, he looked down and simply shook his head, as though in defeat.

"If you want to come down in the morning, we'll talk about it," the officer said pleasantly. "I don't suspect you'll be having any trouble from here on out."

Taryn stayed on the porch and watched them drive down the hill, their cars disappearing into the darkness.

"Do you feel better?" Julian asked from behind her.

"No," she responded without turning around.

"Why not?"

"Because," she pointed, "the fog is gone. Look."

Sure enough, the sky was clear. The moon and stars glowed overhead.

"And that bothers you why?"

"False sense of security," she replied. "I've had it all my life."

TWENTY-EIGHT

Danvers Mental Hospital, RPH (Danvers, Massachusetts)

"*A*nd he isn't talking at all?"

"Not a peep," Taryn replied.

"Maybe you're right," Julian admitted. "Maybe there is something else going on."

Taryn emitted a huge yawn and stretched her arms over her head. She'd been organizing her CDs for over an hour, putting them in order by the ones she thought Julian needed to hear first. She felt responsible for his music education.

"Have you thought more about Christmas?" he asked. "It was always a favorite season of mine."

"I think we should start decorating now," she said.

"Now?"

Taryn smiled. "I am in the Christmas spirit and who knows what will happen in the future? Besides, with the way I'm feeling it will take me weeks to get everything out and up. By then my friends will be here."

"You know I can't do much more than offer moral support," Julian said.

"You *can* accompany me to the creepy cellar," Taryn laughed. "That's help enough."

She hadn't been back since the evening she'd seen the girl, who was Delilah yet wasn't, in the rocking chair. Taryn hadn't told Julian about that incident; she was afraid it would upset him. If it had been her daughter, she knew that such a story would upset *her*.

"I shall meet you down there, if you'd like to go now," Julian said.

Sarah's boxes of Christmas decorations were stacked against the closest wall. Julian was waiting when Taryn arrived. "There's a lot of them," he said, gesturing to the cartons, tubs, and boxes.

"Sarah liked Christmas a lot, from what I remember. Do you remember her decorating?"

"I have impressions of it," he said. "Perhaps some memories of Christmas music. I am rather fond of that."

"Well, there we go," Taryn laughed. "Some middle ground. We can bond over 'Silent Night.'"

She made five trips between the basement and back hall, carrying as much as she could without injuring herself. Julian remained in the cellar each time, patiently waiting for her to return for more.

"I think you should stop for the night," he cautioned her after the last trip. "You're starting to look peaked."

Indeed, sweat was dripping down her face and her hips were starting to throb. "One more," Taryn declared. "And I'll see you upstairs."

When she bent down to pick the last crate up, however, a slender book fell out. "That doesn't look like decorations," he pointed.

Taryn set the crate down and opened it up. It was full of receipts, loose papers, and envelopes. "Looks like this got brought down here by accident," Taryn said. "Should be up in the attic with the rest of Sarah's things."

When she picked up the small book, her eyes widened.

"What is it?" Julian asked, drawing nearer.

"It's a journal," Taryn replied. "Look."

She held open the first few pages. They were dated 1980. "Bring it with you," he commanded. "You need to sit down and rest."

Taryn nodded her head numbly. Maybe she'd finally get some answers.

*   *   *

"IT'S CLOSE TO MIDNIGHT, TARYN," Julian complained. "Are you sure you want to go out there alone?"

"It's just my car," she laughed. "Well, my rental anyway. "I left my medicine. I'll be right back. You can stand right there and watch me."

"I'll go with you," he muttered.

"I'm not a baby, I'll be fine."

There were only fifty feet between her porch and her car. It wouldn't take her long to jog out there and back. Still, Taryn could feel Julian's eyes on her as soon as she stepped off the porch. He wouldn't follow her, since she'd told him not to, but he'd still watch her. His concern was palpable.

Taryn reached her car without any trouble. She wasn't loving the rented Corolla but until hers was fixed, it if *could* be fixed, she was stuck with it. Now she was wishing she hadn't replaced the transmission last spring. Wasted money, it was.

The night was unnaturally still. It was another clear one and the full moon shone bright overhead. Taryn opened the driver's side door and leaned across the seat to open the middle console. She'd stuck her medicine bottles in there when she'd gone into the police station that morning. She was still thinking about Larry, and the dead way he'd watched her from the police cruiser, when she straightened and started to close the door.

The heavy stick brought down over the back of her neck made a loud "thwack". As Taryn melted to the ground in a sea of blackness, her pill bottles scattered to the wind.

I'm going to have to get refills for those, was the last thing she thought.

TWENTY-NINE

Newport, Rhode Island, RPH

*T*aryn's body was wracked with pain.

There was something covering her head and something hard beneath her and, for a moment, Taryn had the terrorizing sensation of being buried alive. When she reached up to frantically brush the dirt from her face, however, she found herself touching a blanket. She was on her living room floor. Someone had covered her with an afghan.

Her vision still cloudy, Taryn struggled to sit up and look around. The room was fuzzy and there was no depth to her vision.

"Lay back down," a harsh voice barked. It sounded very far away, yet she knew it had to be right on top of her.

Confused, but obedient, Taryn fell back to the floor. Her back and neck were hurting like crazy. She thought she might have twisted or sprained her ankle on the way down too.

"Just," the voice commanded again, "don't say anything."

"I wasn't talking," Taryn grumbled.

She was rewarded by a swift kick in the kneecap.

"Bloody hell!" Taryn shouted. She tried to rise again but was too weak.

Where was Julian, she thought. This would be a most excellent time for him to come out.

"You ruined my entire life," the voice whined.

As Taryn's vision grew clearer, her hearing did as well. The footsteps that paced back and forth in front of her face slowly came into view. The black saddle shoes and voice belonged to a woman.

"I haven't known you long enough to have ruined your life," Taryn retorted. "Bridget."

"Shut up!"

Taryn closed her eyes, gathered her strength, and rolled onto her back. Her nurse towered above her, a pillar of scorn and anger. Her short hair was wild and sprouted from her head like a troll doll. Her mouth, usually all smiles, was contorted into an ugly sneer. She took turns glaring hatefully down at Taryn on the floor and walking to the window where she'd stop and look out.

"Someone's here," she snapped. "I saw them on the porch."

"Nobody's here," Taryn said. "You know I live alone and don't have a social life."

"You saying I'm crazy?"

"Is that a fair question, considering the situation?"

"My life was meant to be different," she said mildly, almost reasonably. "And it would have been, if not for *you*."

Taryn attempted to sit up again, this time easing gently so as not to provoke her assailant's wrath.

"You're going to have to be a lot clearer about this," Taryn said. "I honestly have no idea what you're talking about. Are you the one that slashed my tires? Terrorized me here at the house? Messed up my brakes and steering? Tried to suffocate me in my sleep?"

"Don't mess with me." At this last part, Bridget stopped and turned sharply to face Taryn. "You would've done the same."

"Maybe," Taryn agreed. "But I have to know why."

"My mother had a good job. She was doing well, better than she'd never done. And then your bitch of an aunt fired her," Bridget spat. "And for what? Making a few of the bad kids sit in the dark? Make them talk about what their daddies did to them at night in front of the class? Trust me, she could have done a lot worse. She *did* a lot worse at home."

Ah, Taryn thought. *Well, now we know who "Cloud" was.*

"Bunch of whiney babies," Bridget continued. "Crying to their parents, crying to your aunt."

"She could have found another job."

"Not with what your aunt wrote," Bridget spat. "She couldn't find anything. Six months later found her with her pills in the bathtub. The same pills you take, isn't *that* a kick in the head? The state called her crazy after that and wouldn't let her work. Years of education, years of being highly regarded in the community, and it all came down to a crazy check."

Taryn didn't know what to say. "I'm sorry" didn't seem like it would cut it.

Where *was* Julian?

Bridget stomped back over to where Taryn was now sitting cross-legged on the floor. "And Daddy. *Daddy.* He wouldn't have done it if not for Sarah. He and Mom were fine, fine! The pills made her worse. He was *happy.* It's your family's fault he's dead."

What did I have to do with it? Taryn thought, now feeling slightly miffed.

"I thought your dad died from a heart attack?" Taryn offered helpfully.

"A heart attack after he drove his car off the bridge," Bridget shrilled.

"I am so sorry that this happened to your family," Taryn said slowly. She very gingerly began rising from the floor, not breaking eye contact with Bridget. "I'm sorry about your mom's job and about your dad's, uh, accident."

Although, Taryn said silently to herself, *it doesn't sound like* Mama *was that stable to begin with.*

"But that didn't have anything to do with me. It didn't!"

Bridget continued to shoot darts of hate at her.

"I know you're angry with Sarah, but that wasn't *me.* Sarah's gone now and your mother is still here."

She was standing at her full height now, just feet from where Bridget stood by the window. Although her back and

299

legs were throbbing, she thought she could make it to the front door. She might lose Bridget in the woods if she ran fast enough. If she just had her phone...

Taryn looked around wildly. *Her phone.* It had been there earlier, she was sure of it. Right there on the little table at the end of the sofa. There was no sign of it now.

"It *did* have to do with you," Bridget hissed.

Then, in one swift movement, she stuck her hand behind her back and brought out Taryn's little pistol. With shaking hands, she brought it up to her chest and pointed it at Taryn. "Why do you think Daddy drove off that bridge?"

"He was upset about something?" Taryn ventured.

"He was upset about you!"

"But I didn't even *know* your father," Taryn protested. She inched backwards but Bridget was right upon her like snake.

"*Our* father," she corrected.

"Huh?"

"'Sarah is the love of my life,'" Bridget quoted. "'Without her, I don't want to be alive. My real family is gone. I have no reason to live.' That was what he wrote in his letter to us when he left the house that day. *I* didn't count! My brother didn't count. Not my mother. Just you! You and Sarah. And *she* wouldn't have him!"

Taryn was speechless. "I didn't know, I swear I didn't know!"

The gun in Bridget's hand was violently shaking. "You ruined my life, you and your aunt. I have nothing, *nothing!*"

"You have me," Taryn told her quickly. She made as though to move forward, to touch Bridget's hand, but the other woman roared with fury.

"*Stay back!*"

"What for?" Taryn nearly shouted in return. "You're going to kill me anyway!"

"You have to suffer like I did," Bridget screamed again.

"Ha!" This time Taryn did should. "You think I don't suffer? You think I don't wake up every day feeling like crap? You think I know days without pain? You think my life is just a bouquet of roses?"

Bridget didn't flinch.

"My mother didn't want me! My whole family is gone! My fiancé went out for a ride and went up in flames! I'm dying!" Taryn screeched. "You really think anything you can do will make it *worse*?!"

"Then let me put you out of your misery," Bridget retorted sarcastically.

Later, Taryn wouldn't exactly remember what happened first. The gun fired once but Taryn was already on the ground. Unseen hands had given her a shove. Then Bridget had screamed, a different kind of sound this time. Taryn had seen her, eyes wide with terror, right before she ran from the room. She would remember the sound of the gun as it thudded on the floor and slid over to where she lay, would remember hearing footfalls on the porch. She couldn't know whether they were Bridget's or the police. Someone had dialed 911 not long after Taryn was dragged into the house. The caller hadn't identified themselves, but the officers had heard the entire exchange.

THIRTY

Hawkins-Hagan House, RPH (Richmond, Kentucky)

"***A****re you sure you don't want me* to stay out here with you until your friend arrives?"

Taryn glanced up from the box of ornaments and smiled. "I think I'm okay now," she replied. "Now that I know what was going on."

"I've known Bridget's family for a very long time," Charaty said. "I wouldn't have expected that. Not from *her* anyway."

"She said that her mom has mental health issues," Taryn said.

Charaty snorted. "And Santa Claus has a busy schedule on Christmas Eve."

"The police said that she's been committed twice."

Charaty nodded and hung a colorful ball on the tree. Taryn was loving her parlor. It smelled like cinnamon and pine. "She was crazy long before your aunt had her fired from the school district. I suppose, in hindsight, that it's not extraordinary to think that it was passed down."

"Bridget said that we have the same father," Taryn told her. "It doesn't seem like my aunt would have cheated with a married man."

"Don't judge her too harshly," Charaty said. "I knew Taylor. He was a fine man. If he cheated on his family, there was more to it than you and I will ever know."

Taryn opened her mouth to speak but Charaty cut her off. "And don't beat yourself up over the letter. Nobody's ever seen it but that family. The story has changed over the years. Who knows what it *really* said."

Taryn closed her mouth again.

Charaty hung a sparkly angel from a middle branch and then stepped back and studied the tree. "I don't think we'll be winning any decorating awards but it's awfully colorful."

Taryn walked over to where her housekeeper stood and smiled. The tree was full of glass balls, angels, snowmen, reindeer, and Muppets characters. It had no particular design or theme to it but, as Charaty said, it was colorful. "I like it."

The women laughed.

"Now I'm going out of town so it will be four days before I come back," Charaty warned her. "Try not to make a mess of my work."

"I promise," Taryn swore.

And then, to her surprise, the other woman leaned over and wrapped her arms around Taryn's shoulders. When she pulled back, she had tears in her eyes. "Take care," she whispered.

"I'll be fine," Taryn promised.

* * *

"YOU READY?"

Taryn nodded. "Yep."

"What if there's something in there you don't like?"

305

Taryn patted the cushion next to her. Julian sat and turned his body towards her.

"Then I'll be upset, but at least I'll *know*," Taryn said.

She held Sarah's journal firmly in her hands. The cover was mildewed from the dampness and it was so dirty that it was difficult to tell what its original color had truly been. But the interior might hold answers to some of the questions Taryn had carried for a very long time.

"Let's do this," she smiled.

THIRTY-ONE

November 3

The sabbatical has been a godsend. Luckily, with a reputation for being a recluse, nobody has cared or noticed that I rarely venture outside of the house anymore. At some point, I will have to explain but, for now, I am content keeping my sacred secret to myself. Mother is elated, of course. Rosie could care less but she did send me a card. I suppose she's trying. There are days when I wish we were closer but I know that will never be.

November 20

Sleep has not come easily lately. I read about it in my book and it seems that insomnia is prevalent in pregnancy. But do others suffer such vivid nightmares? Last night I was certain I was being held down in my bed, unable to move. Someone or something had restrained me. For a moment, I was unable to breathe. I woke up panting and terrified.

November 23

I know many women complain about the vomiting and upset stomach but I don't mind it, not really. Each time I find myself in the restroom I remind myself of the purpose. I am terribly excited.

November 30

I expected my life to be much different at this point. I didn't think I would be going through this alone. I am not frightened, but I am rather sad. It is possible that things will change in the future. When his divorce finalized, I thought that would be the end to everything, that we would be able to move forward as responsible adults. Her first suicide attempt soon followed, however. I can understand his hesitancy and I see the responsibility he feels he has. I will be fine. Once he helps her get the help she needs, we will do our best to start anew.

December 5

The noises are keeping me up at night. I find myself moping around the house, unable to sleep or rest. I dream of dying, of the baby dying. I've never been scared in my own home before.

December 11

Sometimes the loneliness is almost unbearable. I should travel to Tennessee to spend the holidays with my parents but I cannot. I am too ill. I haven't gained a single pound yet. Indeed, I have lost almost twenty. I look in the mirror and don't recognize myself.

December 13

I received a death threat in the mail today. Taylor said he would take care of it. I have a feeling she has been coming here at night. I found the rocking chairs disturbed the other morning. I've seen footprints on the porch and in the garden. They must be hers. Sometimes, at night, I hear singing and laughter. I've been locking the doors.

December 24

Merry Christmas to me. The best part of this Christmas is knowing that, in a year, I'll have someone else to share it with. We will be strong, Baby and I. We'll be one another's best friend. I don't need anyone else.

December 27

Some days I feel as though someone is watching me. I hesitate to even go outside anymore. I am jumping at every little sound.

January 4

It's interesting that while I am feeling so down and blue, the rest of the community is experiencing good tidings. So much good news lately. New businesses going in, a new school being built, and someone in Lewisboro won the lottery. Why, when everyone else is joyous, must I be so sad?

January 11

I felt someone watching me again today. There was a darkness inside my heart that made me shudder. I've never felt so alone, or so scared. I'm not afraid for me, but for the little one. I have the burning desire to protect it and I am not sure I know how.

January 20

Another death threat today. She showed up at my house and I had to call the police. It was all so embarrassing. I actually had to pull my gun out at her. She seemed surprised.

February 1

Today I learned I am having a baby girl. I've named her Taryn. Oh, Taryn, please hurry and get here soon.

February 13

Taylor has tried to come over several times but I've kept him away. I am afraid of what she might do. I miss him terribly but my loyalty is to Taryn. Nothing matters but her.

February 16

Sadness. Deep sadness inside of me. I don't know where it's coming from. The newspaper was full of good news for our high school basketball team. Death rates were down for last year. And yet all I want to do is cry. It must be hormones.

February 20

I met other women at the doctor appointment today. They all looked so much better than me. Their swollen bellies and shiny hair and big smiles. I am pale and weak and look sickly.

February 24

I could not get out of bed this morning. Too sick to move.

February 28

Something pushed me walking to the bathroom. Or, more likely, I simply lost my balance. Rosie is afraid I am hurting the baby, that I don't want Taryn. How could that be? She's the only light in the world right now.

March 4

The world is a tunnel of darkness. My bureau is full of notes from her, ways describing my death and Taryn's. I would leave for Nashville if I could. I am deathly afraid that I cannot do this. There's something in my head not quite right.

March 7

I was not meant to be a mother. I was never supposed to be. This is wrong. I can't protect my child. I am unable to even take care of myself.

March 10

Something wants Taryn. This is not me. I don't even recognize myself anymore. I feel like I am slowly going out of my mind. Every second I'm awake I feel something reaching its angry claws to snatch her away from me. Do all mothers feel this way?

March 13

Mother is concerned. She and Rosie are coming here.

March 16

Taryn is here. The world exploded with light and goodness.

March 20

Mother and Rosie are right. There is something wrong. I have been admitted to the hospital. Taryn will be returning with them until I am better.

March 30

Nobody will believe me but Mother. They will think I am crazy. I am <u>not</u> crazy. When Mother left me this house she said that it was duty to take care of it and everything that entails. I understand that now. Taryn must not be here, but I must. I must stay to protect my baby. You can't escape destiny and, for better or for worse, it's my destiny to remain. Taryn will be cared for. My heart is breaking but I feel stronger than I've ever felt. I know what I must do.

Goodbye, my darling.

THIRTY-TWO

"*D*o you think Aunt Sarah was crazy?"

"Do *you*?"

"No," Taryn replied. "I feel it too. You know we both have. There is something here."

"She was protecting you," Julian said softly. "Either from herself or from Bridget's mother. She thought she was doing something good. She was probably right."

Taryn sighed and closed her eyes. She had so many questions. What had really happened with her father? What had Sarah known? Why had her other mother agreed to take her on? She wanted to lean over on Julian, to rest her head on his shoulder. To be so close and not be able to touch...it was ripping her in half.

"I need to talk to you," Taryn said at last.

"Yes?"

"The painting. If I finish it, I'll go back. Every time I work on it, I have the dream. One more time and I'll be able to return. You could send a letter with me. We could hide it somewhere in the house. When I see you, I'll give it to you. Then you'll know not to let Delilah sleep in that room or you'll stay up and catch Warwick. Something," Taryn pleaded with him. "Anything. Just let me help."

"We've talked about this," Julian said gently. His head bent as close to hers as he could get. "What if it changes things here? What if–"

"I don't care," Taryn protested stubbornly. "No more what ifs. I don't care about anything but helping you and Delilah."

"I just don't know…"

"Julian, why was Delilah in the other room that night?" She'd asked before but he hadn't given her a clear answer.

"Because I thought I saw her mother in her bedroom earlier that afternoon," he sighed. "I thought it was a sign that something bad would happen in there."

"Remember, Julian, that was me. You saw *me* in her bedroom…"

His eyes grew wide with the realization. "We *did* change something."

"Yes, we did."

It might mean he remarried, fell in love with someone else. That she would never meet him here in this house or that Sarah would even live here. Taryn was willing to risk these things, if it meant that Julian lived.

"Then alright," he said at last. "If it's what you want."

"It's what I want," she smiled. "But you have to recite the letter to me and make sure there are things in it that only you would know. That way the *you* in the past will know that I mean business."

"I'll work on it," Julian laughed.

"And *I'll* work on the painting!"

Taryn spent the afternoon up to her elbows in oil paint and linseed oil. She painted quickly, but took extra care with the detail work. She went back over the bricks in places, making sure that they looked newly placed and fresh. The windows sparkled clean. Wisps of smoke drifted from the chimneys. Colorful flowers unfurled in the sunlight, their velvety petals soft enough to touch. The extra wing was there in all its glory, not a mark on it. A wooden swing fell from a maple tree and seemed to blow back and forth gently in the breeze. Steps to the front door held the slightest imprint of footprints, as though someone had recently trod them. The door was slightly open, shadows peeking through the vestibule. In the background, the barn rose tall and proud. Julian's prize horses grazed peacefully in the lush, green grass. An English saddle was balanced on a fence rail.

"It's magnificent," Julian said proudly. "I couldn't love it more than if I'd done it myself."

Taryn laughed. "You have zero modesty."

"You should always be proud of your work," he lectured her.

"Do you have your letter ready?" she asked.

"It's in my mind."

"Then let's start–"

Taryn was cut off by the ringing of her telephone.

"Miss Magill? This is Lieutenant Masterson."

Taryn was not overly surprised. They'd said they'd get back to her with any new developments. "Hi there. How are you?"

"Well, I am doing okay. How are you these days?"

"Better," Taryn grinned, "now that nobody's trying to kill me. Do you have any news?"

"We do," he told her. "Mr. Stevenson was released last night. I wanted to let you know. We didn't have a reason to keep him. No evidence he'd done anything wrong besides sneaking around your barn. We charged him with trespassing and you're free to pursue that."

"So why was Larry up here?" Taryn asked.

"He couldn't say. Said he woke up as we were putting him in the cruiser. Claims he has no memory of being there at all."

This news *did* surprise Taryn. "And Bridget? Did she admit to everything she did?"

"Well, that's another thing," the Lieutenant said slowly. "She admitted to slashing your tires, assaulting you, and breaking your windows. But she claims that she didn't attack you in your sleep, do anything to your brakes and power steering, or that she was responsible for harassing you that night with the doors."

"Huh."

"Miss Magill, is there anyone else that might want to bother you?"

"I don't think so," she replied. "But then, I didn't think Bridget wanted to either so..."

By the time she hung up the phone, Taryn was feeling disheartened. "We can't blame it all on Bridget," she sighed.

"I'm sorry," Julian said.

"Well, let's keep going," Taryn said, forcing her voice to be cheerful. "Let's hear your letter."

She sat down with a pen and sheet of paper and waited while he dictated the letter that would hopefully save his life.

*　　*　　*

"I'm feeling ready for this," Taryn proclaimed. She stood at the foot of her bed, in her white cotton nightgown, and looked at Julian with hopeful eyes. "Are you?"

"I don't know," he replied honestly. "I know that I can't hang around here forever but it hasn't been so bad so far..."

Taryn giggled. When Julian's face remained sober, however, she stopped.

"I am worried about us," he admitted. "I am worried that I will never see you again."

"I know," Taryn replied quietly. "So am I. I–I don't even know what to say at this point."

"This makes little sense," Julian whispered.

"It doesn't."

Taryn took a step towards Julian and raised her hand. He did the same. Although their fingers were touching, Taryn felt like she was pressing on nothing but hot wind. She could see his fingers close in around hers, but she felt only warmth, not pressure.

Now, surprising herself, she felt nervous. He studied her with serious eyes, his head cocked to one side as though trying to remember everything about her face.

"Forney," she whispered.

Suddenly the air was filled with fire. Taryn was tossed backwards and flew across the room, her back ramming into the nightstand behind her. Julian flew the other way and then dissipated.

Taryn fought against the wind. Staggering to her knees, she began to crawl towards the edge of the bed where she could grab hold of the post and pull herself up. Her hair blew straight back from her head. The gale that threatened to consume her was putrid and thick. Taryn retched and, upon opening her mouth, her throat was assaulted by the decay that accompanied the airstream.

This was no spirit, Taryn thought to herself, this was something much bigger. Much *worse*.

She knew that it wasn't human, had never been human. Knew that it wanted her and probably always *had*. Her mother had been right. Still, though Taryn was afraid, she pulled herself tall and wrapped her arms around the post.

She only had one weapon in the world that she could use to fight such a thing.

"Julian!" she cried.

He was beside her, then, on the other side of the post. The squall flattened his curls and his eyes reflected her horror. Whatever it was that encircled them howled and roared. Taryn felt her nightgown torn and shredded. Long, deep scratches slashed down her legs. Still, she held on.

Then she freed a hand. "Look at me," she shouted over the din.

With their eyes locked, Julian held out his hand as well. When they met in the middle, the light between them grew until it had engulfed Taryn, filling her with warmth from head to toe. One more powerful gust whipped through them and for a second Taryn felt his hand on hers.

Then the room was quiet and they were alone. Her nightgown's hem dropped back to the floor. Pieces of it were scattered all over the room. Trickles of blood ran down her legs.

All she could remember was the feel of his hand.

THIRTY-THREE

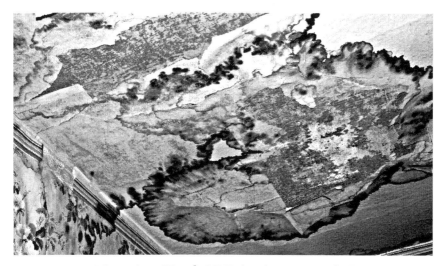

Riverview Hotel, RPH (Irvine, Kentucky)

"*I won't do it.*" Julian stomped around the room, his face hard and stubborn. "I won't let you."

"You can't stop me," Taryn shot back.

"I can and I will," Julian said.

"Why don't you want me to?" she pleaded.

"Because you'll get hurt."

Taryn stomped her foot on the bedroom floor. "You don't know that."

"I am not going to let you return with me. We don't even know that it will work!"

Taryn shrugged. "I was going back anyway. Why not just stay? Come on, think of it. I have one chance, one opportunity to try. Why can't I just be there? With you and Delilah?"

Julian spun around and glared at her. "Give me one reason why going back is better than being here."

"*You*," she retorted.

His face softened and he smiled. "Well, be that as it may...I need another."

"I don't hurt there," she began. "It could be that I don't even have EDS in the past."

"But..."

"And I have nothing here! They have me waiting around to die. I lost my career, I never see my friends...With you and Delilah I could have the chance at a life! A *real* life," she said passionately. "Let me come back and be with you two."

"No."

Taryn felt her heart dropping. "Why not?" she asked quietly. "Why do people keep letting me go?"

Julian's face fell. "Oh, can't you see it has nothing to do with that? Do you not realize that I would literally walk through as many time periods as I had to to be with you?"

"We can do this," she persisted.

"We can, but you shouldn't."

"I don't understand."

"Taryn," Julian said gently. "Don't you remember the dates?"

"What dates?"

"The dates of the community, when things happened. The period of good times."

"I remember," she shrugged. "So?"

"They coincide with Nora's life," he smiled sadly.

"I know," Taryn agreed. "I put that together too. Your wife seemed to have something that kept whatever this nastiest is at bay. As long as she was here, things were pretty much okay. The fires, the tornadoes, earthquakes, people going nuts—all of that seem to go on before she was born and after she died. I noticed it to."

"They coincide with Nora's life," he repeated. "And *yours*."

Taryn was stunned. Not once had she thought of *that*. As she quickly ran the dates through her mind again, however, she realized he was right.

"But..."

"I don't know what's here. I don't know if it's something that comes from the lake, if it's something in the ground. Maybe it's the devil himself," Julian said, "but, whatever it is, it needs *you* to counteract it. That's why it's been attacking you, been trying to drive you off. Whatever it is you have inside of you, it's afraid of it. It can't have you here so you *must* be here!"

"I don't–"

"When you're here, things are better. Your aunt knew it. She knew it was after you because it was afraid of you. She sent you away because you weren't strong enough yet."

"And she brought me back because you can't fight destiny," Taryn finished. She finally understood. "I had to stop coming because something must have happened on that last visit. Maybe when she got pushed in the pond? She knew it wasn't time yet. I wasn't ready. I don't understand though. I am not that good. I am not a nice person most of the time."

"Well," Julian said lightly. "I kind of like you."

She smiled weakly. "Why me?"

"Isn't there a chance that the entire reason you can see through your camera is because you're special? Because you have something that nobody else has? Maybe it was preparing you."

"I don't know..."

"Think about it, Taryn. You have a special connection with time. Time doesn't seem to affect you," Julian said. "You're almost able to *control* it. You move through it, you're constantly aware of it, you can envision it. The past, the present, the future–none of it seems to exist for you. You're constantly living in all of them at once."

"But if I went back…"

"Taryn." Julian walked over to her and stood as close as he could. "Those nights when you dreamed of the house? I couldn't find you. I couldn't come here because you weren't here."

"I don't understand."

"If you go back, it's not just that you'll suddenly disappear from here," he said, "it might be as though you were never here to begin with. You might cease to exist, except with me in mine."

Taryn began to cry. She dropped down to the bed and buried her head in her hands. "Does it matter?" she sobbed.

She could feel him lower himself to her side. "What would it do to the people that loved you if you were never here? To your grandmother? To Sarah? What would their lives have been like? What about Matt? Think about him. Would his life be different if not for you?"

Taryn remembered Matt telling her that he never would have sought out aeronautical engineering if not for her encouragement. Neither had friends in school. Would he have been alone without her? Had she truly made a difference in his life?

"The jobs you've worked, the people you've helped," Julian continued. "All of that reversed."

She thought of the missing teenager in Georgia. Nicki and Shawn in Wales. Her teacher friend in Kentucky. Liza Jane and Bryar Rose. What was fate anyway? Was she an active part of it or would the chips have fallen the same way anyhow, even without her presence?

"It's too big a chance to take," Julian said gently. "We can't take it."

"But I *really* love you," she sniffed. "And not just because you're dead and you disappear and leave me alone a lot."

Julian laughed from the bottom of his stomach, a booming sound that mound Taryn smile through her tears. "And I love you as well, but this isn't over," he said softly. "Do you think I believe that? I still believe there *is* a way. I refuse to believe that we went through all of this, that I have waited for more than a century, to simply say goodbye now."

"If I go back and help you then I am dead," she said slowly. "But if I don't then you're dead. Who's the winner in this situation? Is there a way at all?"

"I don't know," Julian said. "I just want *you.*"

Taryn suddenly found herself feeling very tired. The ache that had started in her stomach when she'd flown into the nightstand was now spreading to her back.

"I need to lie down," she said.

He moved over and made room for her. As she stretched out on the bed, her mind was going a hundred miles an hour. Then there was a spark, a flicker. Something clicked. And she knew.

"Do you trust me?" she asked at once. "I need to make this decision and I feel like I need to make it *soon*. The painting might only give me one chance."

"I trust you," he replied gravely.

"I'm very tired," Taryn yawned.

"It's been a long week," Julian agreed.

"You really think this isn't over?" she asked sleepily. Taryn turned on her side, trying to find a comfortable position, and studied Julian through weary eyes.

"Do you trust *me*?" he asked gently.

She nodded that she did but he suddenly looked very sad. She wanted to hug him but, of course, she couldn't.

She'd made her decision, however. It had come upon her quickly. In the end, she hadn't even had to think about it much.

"Will you stay with me for awhile? Until I go to sleep?"

"Of course." Julian stretched out beside her. They were almost nose to nose.

He is always so warm, Taryn thought. The other thing, the darker thing, had been so cold.

Taryn closed her eyes. "Will you sing to me?" she asked slyly.

"Of course," he grinned.

"Good night Julian." The pillow was soft against her cheek. She could almost smell her mother.

"*Irene goodnight...*"

EPILOGUE

"Thanks, Charaty, I appreciate it."

Back straight and hair neatly in place, Charaty resembled an old-fashioned school marm.

"You're welcome," she replied. "If you'd like, I'll wait here in the foyer. I didn't know if you'd..."

Nicki reached out and clasped Charaty's hand in hers. "I would, actually, if you don't mind."

"Sometimes people don't want to be alone," Charaty added.

Nicki slowly traversed the first floor of the old, stone house. Everything looked so beautiful, all ready for Christmas. Taryn had done a good job. Nicki stopped at different places, taking in and smiling at the furniture and accessories that Taryn had picked out. She'd clearly spent a lot of time taking special consideration with everything she'd brought into her aunt's house.

"What do you plan on doing, if you don't mind my asking?" Charaty called from the foyer.

"My husband and I are going to come back in a month and stay here for awhile," Nicki answered. "She left plenty to get us through the first year. I had no idea that Taryn was good with money."

"Miss Taryn was a special kind of person," Charaty reported stiffly.

"Yes," Nicki called over her shoulder, "she was."

"Well, if you need a housekeeper while you're here..."

Nicki paused in front of the CD stand and found herself tearing up at once. Tift Merritt, Allison Moorer, Kelly Willis, Iris Dement...seeing all of Taryn's favorite musicians one right after the other brought a pang to her heart. She couldn't believe that she'd never hear another lecture from her on alternative country music, never cook in a kitchen while Taryn danced around with the spatula and sang off-key.

"I left the bedroom as it was," Charaty said from behind her. "I thought you might want to be the one to..."

"Yes," Nicki nodded as she wiped away a tear and smiled. "I want to see it."

"I need to step outside for a moment but I'll be right back. It's the room at the top of the stairs."

As Nicki started up the staircase, however, she heard Charaty call her name again. When she turned and looked at her, Charaty wore a strange expression.

"I don't know if I should be telling you this or not but," she paused and her face turned red. "I was the one to find Miss Taryn. She was in bed. I knew what had happened right away. But she looked like an angel."

"They said that she passed away very quickly," Nicki said with a hitch in her voice. "And that she didn't suffer any pain."

Thank God, she added to herself. When the aneurysm had ruptured, it had happened quickly. The coroner said Taryn had probably not even been aware of what was going on at the time.

"Yes," Charaty agreed. "But when I walked into the room and went up to the bed, it was what I saw beside her that had me confused."

"Yeah?" Nicki asked. "What was that?"

"The bed was made but on the opposite side it had been rumpled, as though someone else had been there. And an indention in the pillow right beside her," Charaty added. "It looked as though…"

"Yes?"

"As though someone else was there with her." Charaty laughed a nervous chuckle. "The original owner of this house died in a fire with his daughter. I often wondered if he haunted the place. Maybe he was looking after her."

When Nicki reached the bedroom, she could hear the closing of the front door. Charaty, she saw from the window, was outside in the driveway.

Oh Taryn, Nicki thought with a sob. *I am so sorry. I should have been here.*

She took two laps around the bedroom, carefully running her fingers over Taryn's clothes, so little and so cute, hanging neatly in the wardrobe and her perfume bottle on the bureau. She frowned at the sight of a wadded-up nightgown in the corner and then replaced it, confused, when she saw that it was torn.

At the bed, Nicki paused. She tried to imagine Taryn lying down for the last time. All alone and maybe scared. And yet...

The house felt *good*. Nicki was sure of it. Shawn had commented on the town as they'd driven through Lewisboro. "I like it here," he'd said. "It has a good feel to it."

Miss Dixie beckoned her from the nightstand and Nicki picked the camera up now and cradled it in her hands.

She was halfway across the landing, Taryn's camera clutched like a treasure, when she stopped in her tracks. For a moment, she was certain she heard the rolling notes of a waltz floating up from downstairs. The beautiful notes swelled through the house and filled Nicki's heart until it was brimming with happiness. And then, for a fraction of a second, she heard laughter. Laughter from a man and a woman that were exactly where they were supposed to be.

AUTHOR'S NOTE

This preceding book is a work of fiction. With that in mind, there are some truths to it. Here are a few of them...

If you've read my nonfiction book, *A Summer of Fear*, you'll find some similarities. It also takes place in a haunted house in New Hampshire. When I first started writing Sarah's House in 2005, more than ten years ago, it was in that house in New Hampshire. I'd taken my laptop with me with the intentions of getting a lot of work done. Well, life got in the way and I only ended up with about thirty written pages. Still, the seed was planted and I ended up using some of my experiences from that very house.

I actually started writing this book in the fall of 1998. My original idea was to do an updated version of one of my favorite movies, "The Ghost and Mrs. Muir." I always saw it as a love story above everything else. I knew there was more to it, however. I finished the book in 2010 but wasn't happy with it. I felt like it needed a prequel, that we needed to know more about Taryn. Thus, *Windwood Farm* was born. Of course, *Sarah's House* wound up with eight sequels, and not just one.

Some of the places in the book are real. The Kancamagus Highway, for instance, as well as Conway and Portsmouth. Lewisboro is a figment of my imagination, although I based it a little bit off Wolfeboro, which is one of my very favorite small towns. (I call it "Stars Hollow on water.")

In the original story, Taryn had cancer and had just gotten through a bad divorce. She'd taken on the old house as a place to spend the last few months of her life because she wanted to be alone. I eventually changed that to EDS because it's something that I have and not too many people are aware of it.

Sarah's house is based on a real house. My mother was in college to get her MA and was in class with a woman named Sara Adams. Sara was the principal of Athens-Boonesboro Elementary school in Lexington Kentucky. Her husband, Bill, was in charge of the farms and agricultural campus for the University of Kentucky. His job came with a house–a beautiful old house on the college's farm. It was built in the 1880s.

Sara had a wonderful garden and she would invite us up every summer to come get whatever we wanted. We usually spent a few nights. The house was big, old, and creaky. It didn't have AC and it was not in the best of shapes. I loved it. Spending the weekends there was always a highlight of my summers and falls. After a day in the garden, Sara would cook whatever fresh vegetables she had picked and so the house would smell like corn on the cob and tomatoes. I loved waking up each morning, looking out over the farm from my windows, and pretending I was back in time.

When Bill retired in 1992 they moved from the house and nobody ever lived in it again. I visited a few times after that and the house was looking pretty sad. When I returned to show my kids in 2015, it had been demolished.

I still grieve for that house.

Julian Alderman is not a real person. He is not based on anyone. With that being said, I totally stole his name from a guy I had a crush on back in college. He didn't know I existed.

The character of Taryn's grandmother Stella, who has her own short story, "Stella", is partly based on my own grandmother. The character is based on my maternal grandmother, I was very close to her, but her name is actually that of my paternal grandmother–Stella Morgan.

Matt, who is not in this book but is a major player in the other books in the series, is not based on any one person. I did have two very close male friends in middle and high school and he is a bit of a composite of those boys. Well, up until this book anyway.

Nicki and Shawn, who readers met in *Bloody Moor*, are based on real people in my life–Nicola Dorgan and Sean Hernandez. I met them in Wales a dozen years ago and they're still two of my closest friends (although they are actually married to other people and not to each other).

I am sad to see this series come to an end. However, I really felt like Taryn's story was finishing up. I left a year between the ending of *Bloody Moor* and the start of *Sarah's House* so it's always possible that I will go back through and add a few companion stories here and there to fill in the gaps.

Thanks for reading.
Rebecca

ABOUT THE AUTHOR

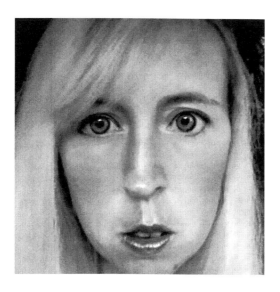

Rebecca Patrick-Howard is the author of several books including the paranormal mystery series *Taryn's Camera*. She lives in eastern Kentucky with her husband and two children. To order copies of ALL of Rebecca's books, including autographed paperbacks, visit her website at:

www.rebeccaphoward.net

OTHER BOOKS BY REBECCA

Taryn's Camera Series

Windwood Farm (Book 1)

The locals call it the "devil's house" and Taryn's about to find out why!

Griffith Tavern (Book 2)

The old tavern has a dark secret and Taryn's camera's going to learn it soon.

Dark Hollow Road (Book 3)

Beautiful Cheyenne Willoughby has disappeared. Someone knows the truth.

Shaker Town (Book 4)

Taryn's camera is finally revealing a past to her that she's always longed to see-the mysterious Shakers as they were 100 years ago. But is she seeing a past she hadn't bargained for?

Jekyll Island (Book 5)

Jekyll Island is known for its ghosts, as well as its fascinating history, but now the two are about to take Taryn on a wild ride she'll never forget!

Black Raven Inn (Book 6)

The 1960's music scene...vibrant, electrifying, and sometimes even deadly...

Muddy Creek (Book 7)

Lucy did a bad, bad thing when she burned down the old school. Now it's up to Taryn to find out why.

Bloody Moor (Book 8)

The call it "the cursed" and the townspeople still fear the witch that reigned there a century ago. But this haunted Welsh mansion has more than meets the eye!

Sarah's House (Book 9)

Taryn's Pictures: Photos from Taryn's Camera

Kentucky Witches

A Broom with a View

She's your average witch next door, he's a Christmas tree farmer with sisters named after horses. Kudzu Valley will never be the same when Liza Jane comes to town!

Broommates

When Bryar Rose makes a fool of herself on national television, it's time for her to return to Kudzu Valley. But now that she's accused of murdering half the town, will anyone truly accept her?

A Broom of One's Own

What does a witch do when she can't get rid of the restless spirit that haunts the old cinema? Call for backup! (A Taryn's Camera/Kentucky Witches crossover)

General Fiction

Furnace Mountain: Or The Day President Roosevelt Came to Town

When Sam Walters invited the president to visit his Depression-era town, he never dreamed of what would happen next!

The Locusts (Coming Soon)

Things She Sees In The Dark (Coming Soon)

Mallory's cousin was kidnapped when she was eight years old and Mallory saw the whole thing happen. She's suffered amnesia ever since. Now, 25 years later, her memories are starting to return. Can she solve the case that no detective has been able to crack? And will she live through it, if she does?

True Hauntings

Haunted Estill County

More Tales from Haunted Estill County

Haunted Estill County: The Children's Edition

Haunted Madison County

A Summer of Fear

The Maple House

Four Months of Terror

Two Weeks: A True Haunting

Three True Tales of Terror

The Visitors

Other Books

Coping with Grief: The Anti-Guide to Infant Loss

Three Minus Zero

Finding Henry: A Journey Into Eastern Europe

Estill County in Photos

Haunted: Ghost Children Stories From Beyond

Haunted: Houses

CONNECT WITH REBECCA!

REBECCA'S LINKS

Pinterest: https://www.pinterest.com/rebeccapatrickh/

Website: www.rebeccaphoward.net

Email: rphwrites@gmail.com

Facebook:
https://www.facebook.com/rebeccaphowardwrites

Twitter: https://twitter.com/RPHWrites

Instagram: https://instagram.com/rphwrites/

KENTUCKY WITCHES

Like THIS series? Meet the Kentucky Witches!

http://www.rebeccaphoward.net/a-broom-with-a-view.html

Liza Jane Higginbotham is your average witch next door. Just a down home girl, she enjoys driving her truck, listening to country music and, oh yes, the occasional brew.

This witch just wants to enjoy the quiet life. When her no-good, hipster husband cheats on her with a tuba player, she moves back to take over the family farm in rural Eastern Kentucky. Here, she's expecting some peace, content to play in her garden, restore the dilapidated farmhouse, and throw her money away at the town auction house every Friday night.

But the town of Kudzu Valley just won't let a witch rest. From the high school football coach looking for a charm to help the team win the Homecoming game to Lola Ellen Pearson who wants to hex the local Pizza Hut for giving her food poisoning the night before her fourth wedding, everyone wants SOMETHING from the town's resident witch!

When Cotton Hashagen's dead body is found, though, all eyes turn to Liza Jane. After all, hadn't she JUST accused the local meter reader of a terrible crime? With the townspeople and police turning their eyes to Liza Jane, it's going to take a lot for her to prove that she didn't put a "whammy" on him AND solve the mystery to find the real culprit!

65592818R00197

Made in the USA
Middletown, DE
01 March 2018